ACE CARROWAY
AND THE
MIDNIGHT SCREAM

GUY WORTHEY

ACE CARROWAY AND THE MIDNIGHT SCREAM

This is a work of fiction. Names, characters, places, and incidents are either the product of the author's imagination or are used fictitiously. Any resemblance to actual persons, living or dead, is entirely coincidental.

Cover design: Kendall R. Hart

Copyright © 2020 Guy Worthey

All rights reserved.

ISBN: 1-949827-50-X
ISBN-13: 978-1-949827-50-7

Westing Press

To Kayla,

ace archaeologist.

BARNSTAPLE, THURSDAY, JUNE 22, 1922.

SALES BY AUCTION.

HERBERT W. COURT, F.A.I.

AUCTIONEER, VALUER, HOUSE,
ESTATE, and INSURANCE AGENT,

PARRACOMBE and BARNSTAPLE.

Monthly Auctions for Live and Dead Stock at
Blackmoor Gate, West Buckland, and Westdown,
and Periodical Auctions at Newton Tracey,
Instow, and Sherwill; also

Weekly Sales in Barnstaple Cattle Market.

Telephone: Parracombe 44 x 2.   Barnstaple 243.

FOR TO-MORROW (FRIDAY), in BARN-
STAPLE CATTLE MARKET:—Bay Mare,
5 years old, quiet in all harness, good Vanner or
Poster, and subject to Vet; Cob, 14-3 h.h., 6
years old, good in all harness.

SALE THIS DAY (THURSDAY), at WEST-
DOWN, for DRAFT STOCK, as previously
advertised—Sale at 2 p.m.
HERBERT W. COURT. F.A.I., Auctioneer.

WEST BUCKLAND MONTHLY AUCTION.

MESSRS. F. DOBBS and HERBERT W.
COURT, F.A.I., will conduct the above
on TUESDAY NEXT, JUNE 27th. Present
Entries:—

280 Fat and Store SHEEP.
40 Fat and Store BEASTS.
Quantity of Gardening Tools, Pig Troughs,
Wheelbarrow, Bee Hives, Pig Stock, Coal Scoop,
Cider Cask, Fire Grate, and other Effects.
Sale at 11.30 a.m.

PARK VILLAS, BRATTON FLEMING.

HERBERT W. COURT, F.A.I., has been
instructed by the Representatives of the
late Mr. W. Burge to Sell by Auction, on SATUR-
DAY, JULY 1st next the whole of the Well-made

HOUSEHOLD FURNITURE,

&c., therein, including Rare Old Oak Chest and
Oak Tallboy Chest of Drawers.
Full particulars in next week's issue.
Sale at 2 p.m. sharp

BLACKMOOR GATE MONTHLY AUCTION.

HERBERT W. COURT, F.A.I., will conduct

HEIRESS ROBBED
IN DARING 2ND STORY HEIST

Celebrated suffragette Mrs. Evelyn
Fitzhugh of Frome called police in a panic
Wednesday night from Fitzhugh Manor.
She reported missing jewelry and other
fantastical elements that brought the
gendarmerie in at a run.

The jewelry, a trove of antique French
items, disappeared from her locked
upstairs room while she was dining with
neighbors. Neither the outside doors nor
the upstairs locks were compromised.
Entry was accomplished by the second
story window, whose lock was broken.

Whoever perpetrated the crime did so
without shoes, reported Constable Norris
of Salisbury. Only bare footprints of small
size were detected in the garden, and no
impressions such as a ladder might make.
This unshod gang of acrobatic women or
children left two-thirds of the jewelry
behind. Moreover, they left a solid gold
cross weighing several ounces in place of
the items they stole.

A stable boy two properties over added a
twist to the tale. He reported seeing four
dark figures in a line like "small naked
monks." These figures prayed their way
across a pasture, then disappeared behind
a hedgerow.

Constable Norris would not comment on
such specifics. He assured reporters that
all aspects of the matter would be
investigated thoroughly.

Chapter 1

The Giant's Dance rose out of the lonely plain as if the mossy monoliths had grown from the ground like colossal cacti. The eye swiveled magnetically to the ancient posts and lintels at first. To look away took effort. Over time, however, the granitic reality of Stonehenge seeped past the eyes into the mind. Eventually, visual confirmation was no longer necessary. The multi-ton stones stood there now, had always stood there, and would always stand there.

Sam Raia Biming, archaeologist, shivered.

No moon graced the midsummer midnight of 1922. The unsettled sky alternated bands of rain-heavy clouds with clear patches. The midnight rituals at the heel stone were over. The druids retired to their fire, well outside the sarsen circle. The witch coven sought their own fire on the opposite side. While low chants and songs rose and fell, the separate bonfires dimmed to embers. According to their separate but parallel traditions, witch and druid would rouse again before dawn to greet the first sun of the new season.

As regards regular tourists, only a few chilled, wet individuals remained. Most had fled after midnight to warm beds and sweet slumber.

Undetected by any, black shadows flowed among the standing stones. In purposeful silence they danced.

Outside the mystic circle, posts and ropes cordoned off a section of turf. Sam Biming glanced at the standing stones and shivered anew. He turned to his audience of two, a pair of shadows in the gloom. "We are finding postholes. They are arranged in a much larger circle than the standing stones. No trace of the wood itself remains except for discoloration of the soil."

"Posts?" inquired the tourist, a stout Scottish woman. "As in, fence posts?"

"More robust than that, milady. More like telegraph poles," replied the short, round, dark-skinned Sam. Despite the clammy chill, his manner of speaking remained polite and carefully grammatical. "Likely, they were topped with horizontal timbers, rather like the Stonehenge trilithons."

"So, it was a woodhenge, not a stonehenge?" The tourist laughed.

Sam remained sober. "Yes, milady."

"How old were the posts?" the witch wanted to know. He dressed like a druid in cloak and cowl, but earlier made it known that he was a superior witch, not an inferior druid.

"We are not sure of exact dates, sahib. However, the wood construction came first. The stone construction appears contemporaneous with early Egyptian cultures. That is, about four thousand years old. The woodhenge would have been older still."

A conversational pause descended. All three contemplated the span of four millennia. The dark of night and the clammy humidity seeped into their bones.

Sam spoke on, dreamily, "Stone or wood, the circles were used for keeping track of the calendar. This *particular* stone circle was also a burial site. Many are buried here. If my colleagues are right, uncounted more were cremated and their ashes strewn here. It is a place of death as well as an astronomical observatory."

"Aye? 'Tis a cemetery, ye ken?" blurted the Scottish tourist.

The hooded witch intoned, "Death leads to life, and life leads to death, and we are all on the endless cycle of—"

There came a scream.

It came ragged, raw, and primal. It ripped from some nearby throat in acute mortal agony. The horrific screech might have been human, but it sounded demonic.

Every witch, druid, and tourist leapt to their feet, eyes wild, hands poised for defense. They could not help it. Instinct overpowered all. The scream reduced them to animals. Their hackles raised and their teeth bared. Their heads quested wildly for the source of danger.

But there was nothing to be seen. Their ears told them that the scream had come from the center of the stone circle. Their eyes saw only moving, looming shadows cast by their own dim, flickering fires.

The after-scream silence gave way to a nervous babble.

Sam's voice rose above it. "Build the fires larger, please! We need light."

Sam was the first to step beneath the towering stone monuments into the sarsen circle, scouting cautiously.

Dark, wet splashes painted the jumble of stones nearest the center of the circle. The patches glistened in the firelight. Glossy, black-looking drips crawled down the stones. Sam's mouth slowly dropped open in a frown of growing horror.

A timid crowd gathered behind Sam. As the fire-light grew brighter, Sam knelt. He dipped a finger to one of the stains. The slippery warmth on his fingertip shone a deep, deep red.

Sam's eyebrows jetted upwards and he blurted, "It is blood! Someone has been murdered!"

CHAPTER 2

Dawn arrived gray. The witches and druids clustered in very tight circles, chanting for ritual comfort. Puzzled policemen wandered among the standing stones. Rain threatened. There was no hope of observing the famous sunrise over the heel stone that marked midsummer and the turning of the seasons. But even if the sky had been transparent as glass, not a soul would choose to crouch on the spatter of blood to watch.

A fatigued, chilled, miserable Sam furrowed his brow. His fingers stroked his neat mustache, but the wax had worn away and the curls at the end had gone limp. He glanced up at the policeman next to him. "There is only blood. There is no body. It is as if he who screamed was burst asunder, but the bones lifted into the sky. Or sank into the earth."

"There certainly is a good bit of blood," dourly assented the bobby. He frowned at a grisly scene that looked more and more horrifying as the day brightened. Splashes of crimson rayed outward from the center of the sarsen circle. Grass and stones alike dripped with dark blood, only slightly dulled and browned in the moist hours since the midnight scream.

"'Ere, come 'ave a look!" called another policeman some distance away. He was pointing at a spot on the ground.

Sam and the bobby minced over, trying not to step on the splash marks. The object in the grass glowed with a soft metallic glint. All three bent over, peering intently.

A policeman said, "Doctor Biming, I do believe that bit might lie in your realm of expertise. More than ours, I mean."

Sam bent and extended slow fingers to gather it up. It was unexpectedly heavy for an object so small. Bright links of chain dangled from a loop that formed the top arm of a cross. The whole arrangement gleamed with a rich luster.

He hefted the object and held it close to his eye. "It is an amulet. It appears to be made of elemental gold. Solid gold, many ounces. The short chain seems fitted for the neck of a woman, but tight even so. The style called a 'choker' in English, I believe."

Sam held the amulet high, reverentially. "The amulet is an ankh in overall shape, a cross with a teardrop top. It is perhaps the most common symbol in ancient Egypt, symbolizing the power of life. However, the central carving is of Horus in his falcon shape. The stylized carving is that of early Egyptian dynasties. Horus was a god of the air. Pardon me if I repeat information that is obvious."

The bobbies eyed each other. One of them attempted to scribble notes in a small notebook. The other mumbled, "Naw, guv'nor. Push on."

Sam brought the ankh inches from his eyes. "The carving is quite finely done. Without context, I cannot say how old this artifact is. If it is pure gold, it will not tarnish. It could be thousands of years old or it could have been poured last week. I note that finding a goldsmith capable of making it would be a difficult thing."

Sam blinked up from the golden artifact.

The bobbies stared at him.

Sam grimaced. "I am sorry, sirs. Was I not speaking in the English language? It is an occupational hazard to slip into other languages."

The policemen glanced at each other. The one taking notes said, "You spoke English. Just a bit much for me to jot down."

Sam smoothed the ends of his curled black mustache. "Gentlemen, perhaps I should put my summary in writing for you. If you want the Museum to appraise the piece, I'm sure they would be happy to do that."

"Yeh, all right," said one.

The other said, "Supposing all the while that some crime has been committed, of course. Some crime other than disturbing the peace."

The first said, "And vandalism. If leaving gold treasure and a lot of blood is vandalism."

As if cued by the policeman's remark, a downpour of rain commenced. Soon, the blood would wash away and soak into the earth. And the Giant's Dance would stand as it always had, silent and patient. Stonehenge stood unmoved by either life's beginnings or life's endings.

Sam eavesdropped on the police as they spoke with other witnesses. None of the witches or druids had seen or heard anything more.

Missing an entire night of sleep, Sam nevertheless spent the next day in travel. He journeyed back to London by car, cab, and train. In the station, by reflex of habit, Sam bought a copy of *The Times*. He perused it between naps and one particular article caught his avid attention. He read it three times.

Upon arriving in London, he stopped by the telegram office and dictated a message to C. Carroway & Associates, New York.

POSSIBLE MURDER AT STONEHENGE BUT NO BODY STOP GOLD ANKH AMULET OF HORUS AT SCENE STOP JEWELS STOLEN IN DEVONSHIRE STOP SIMILAR GOLD ANKH AMULET OF ISIS AT SCENE STOP WOULD LOVE HELP WITH MYSTERY IF YOU ARE FREE

His bed was delicious. The exhausted archaeologist overslept and missed the work day at the Museum. He awakened consumed with the mystery of the midnight scream and did not linger over his mustache-grooming. Instead, he bought up all the daily newspapers. Over supper, he read them avidly. The Devonshire theft featured prominently. The victim was an heiress of some fame. Her collection of jewels was notable due to some pre-revolution connections to French royalty. They resided in a locked cabinet, but the lock had been forced overnight. The jewels were gone, and in their place was the solid gold ankh amulet. The Times printed a drawing of it, and Sam recognized Isis, mother of Horus. The reporter called it a clever cat burglary. Entry to the manor had evidently been gained via a second story window. The reporter also mentioned a puzzle: Everything with gemstones was taken but other gold or silver items were left untouched, such as rings, candlesticks, cufflinks, and gold chains.

Sam skipped dessert to check for messages at the telegram office. "Aye," said the visor-wearing operator, and handed over a card with three short words.

ON OUR WAY

Sam's face lit up and he preened his mustache. He sent back his own brief message.

BURGLAR NIMBLE STOP TOOK JEWELS BUT NOT GOLD

The next day, Sam arrived at the Museum early and dragged several reference volumes from the library to his tiny office. The lettering over the door of his cubicle read, "Sam Raia Biming, Research Curator." After an hour of poring over the volumes, Sam rubbed at his temples and closed his eyes. He muttered to himself, "The forms are most similar to statuary found at Thebes, but they are not the same. They are both more antique *and* more modern, simultaneously!"

Restless, Sam quit his chair and swung his short legs to the Egypt wing of the British Museum. The museum had opened. A few early-rising members of the public filtered through the vast halls. Sam directed his steps toward the artifacts from Thebes. He took comfort from the familiar ancient items. They evoked vanished times along the Nile so vividly that Sam could close his eyes and picture scenes from the past.

Today, however, something disturbed his comfort. His eyes roved, seeking whatever had perturbed his tidy sense of order.

There. In a display case of temple relics.

Sam's hand flew to cover the "o" shape of his mouth.

The artifact known as Amun's Helm had vanished. In its place was a small, finely crafted, solid gold amulet in the shape of an ankh. Sam rushed over and stared. The ankh was shaped into the stylized form of a young woman with a tall, flat-topped headdress.

"Nephthys!" Sam breathed.

Chapter 3

The glass of the display case was in perfect order and unmarred. Sam wormed around to the rear and bent to examine the lock. Tool marks and splintered wood met his gaze. Sam's hands became fists.

"Forced!" Sam stroked his curly mustache, but calming himself was out of the question. His hands balled up again, and his round body shook. Amun's Helm was unique. It was irreplaceable. This outrageous crime was an affront to all humanity!

Sam marched off to the guard near the Museum entrance. That guard summoned another, and Sam hissed his story to them. He finished with, "The ankh amulet is like the one left at Stonehenge three nights ago. That one held the likeness of Horus. This one, Nephthys."

A slim man in tweed lounged within hearing distance, quietly puffing on his pipe. He went unnoticed.

Sam's day stretched to a miserable eternity. Between Scotland Yard and the Museum administration, he repeated his story so many times that by the end he knew his own speech by heart. The swirl of his inner anxieties exhausted him more than the whirlwind of people. Images of the Egyptian pantheon intruded on his consciousness. Geb the earth father and Nut the sky mother. Their children, Osiris, Seth, Isis, and

Nephthys. All rambled in his head like puzzle pieces that held great meaning but did not fit together.

Supperless and weary, Sam shuffled out of the museum into the inky night. His first stop was the telegraph office. He fired off another wire to New York, mostly out of frustration.

PLOT THICKENS STOP HELM OF AMUN STOLEN FROM BRITISH MUSEUM AND RE-PLACED BY GOLD ANKH REPRESENTING NEPHTHYS GODDESS OF DEATH

After that, the Egyptologist wandered through fog-wrapped streets, aimless and disconsolate. The thought of bed dimly penetrated his fevered brain, and he squinted at a street sign to try to get his bearings. Lettering grudgingly emerged from the fog. "Temple St."

Sam heaved a long sigh and tapped a finger on his temple. "Fog outside, and fog inside, too." He should be able to deduce what the imagery of the statuettes meant, but the secret eluded him. The gaslights did little to illuminate the dark, empty streets in the dense fog. No other soul seemed about this late. He was alone, yet he heard whispers float upon the night air. Secretive rustlings echoed across glistening cobblestones.

The whispers grew in Sam's mind like looming, flickering shadows cast by a candle flame. He paused to stare into nothingness and mumbled, "Thebes? But the greatest of the gods at Thebes was Amun. There has been no image of Amun, the hidden god." Sam resumed walking. "But how could there be? Amun is everywhere, yet hidden. And his helm is now hidden, too."

"Fff!" a whisper sounded loud. Sam's head whipped to the left. The dark rectangle of an alley framed an inhuman figure. On top, ostrich feathers flanked a tall pale crown. The green oval face below sprouted a dangling black beard. Black arms and legs splayed behind and below, spiderlike.

"Osiris!" Sam mumbled through bloodless lips.

Smooth and silent, the crowned face receded into the gloom of the alley. Its black eyes stared unmoving as darkness covered it.

Sam said, "Osiris! Wait!" He stumbled into the alley after the god. When he arrived, he saw only the dim outlines of rubbish bins and sagging fence gates.

"Seeing things!" he said to himself in Egyptian, his first language. He rubbed his eyes. He cast his eyes around one last time before heading back to the gaslit street—

And movement caught his eye at the far end of the alley. A single, dim electric light dangled there, casting a yellow bubble of light in the fog. At the far edge, a dark figure danced. Female in silhouette, a house-and-basket crown topped her head. The slow swirls of her arm movements flowed like languid waters.

"Nephthys!" Sam said. His feet clattered on the damp cobbles as he ran toward her.

But when he arrived, she had vanished as silently and completely as had Osiris before her.

A glint caught his eye, in the cobblestones ahead of his next footfall.

Sam hopped backward to avoid stepping on it. He knelt. He extended trembling fingers to touch warm metal. The amulet gleamed with the sheen of pure gold, small and heavy. Its short chain could perhaps encircle a petite human neck. Sam's overwrought mind dully accepted the ankh shape and the stylized face carved under the teardrop.

Sam caressed it reverently and whispered, "Seth. Seth, the god of …"

New whisperings and rustlings jolted into Sam's consciousness. He straightened up. Figures surrounded him, silent and looming. "… death."

Their large crowned heads bent slightly to paralyze Sam with a fierce but frozen regard. Part of Sam's mind knew he should run, but the other part was busy with categorizing and sorting. He turned in a circle, breathily reciting as if caught in rapture, "Osiris … Seth … Isis … Nephthys … "

"Ffft!"

Sam felt a sting at his neck. His hand slapped to the spot, and he pulled out a tiny dart.

The archaeologist slipped into Coptic Egyptian as he wobbled, then sank to his knees. "But where … where is Amun, the Hidden God?"

The four figures prowled forward, intent on Sam, their god-masks vivid. The supernatural faces swam and melted together to fill Sam's vision.

Until darkness overcame them all.

Chapter 4

The next day, after the fog had lifted, Croydon Airport air traffic control twiddled its thumbs and gazed at distant pigeons. "Croydon Airport air traffic control" was an underfed, youngish man named Horace Chesterton. He sat surrounded by windows and electrical apparatus in the lonely observation tower. With bored eyes he watched and idly wondered what pigeons found so interesting about the edges of runways.

His vacant expression vanished when the radio crackled to life. A youthful voice with an American accent said, "Croydon Airport. *Sky Arrow One* requesting landing. Over."

Horace Chesterton dropped his feet from the console to the floor and thumbed the transmit switch. "*Sky Arrow One*, identify yourself. Who the devil is this?"

"NX51, Croydon, out of Lark Haven, Pennsylvania, United States. Over."

Horace scribbled the call letters on a pad of paper, then leapt out of his chair to yank a reference volume off the shelf. He flipped pages frantically. His moving finger halted at an entry. "Experimental?" he protested.

A moment later, he gasped. "Dirigible? You must be joking!"

Only then did Mr. Chesterton think to look out the

window into the bright morning. His face went slack and his mouth dropped open.

Operating by sense of touch because his eyes were riveted to the sky, Horace flipped on the public address horns. He spoke into the microphone with a fair semblance of calm. "There's an airship coming!"

Loudspeaker horns scattered over the airfield blared Chesterton's message. All eyes scanned the skies, then focused West. The stately dirigible from America glided toward the airfield. Everyone gawked at the majestic sight.

No one moved, transfixed by the stately grace of the floating behemoth, brilliantly golden with the light of morning. Its sleek shape sliced through the atmosphere with ease. Its speed diminished and its transmitter crackled again. "Croydon, did you copy that?"

Mr. Chesterton switched microphones and fumbled for the send switch. "Copy, NX51! Erm, welcome to London."

Eventually, Horace tore his eyes from the airship to the idle gawkers on the field. He thumbed the public address horn again. "Somebody flag it in, all right? Put it by hangar number two. I guess."

Down on the ground people scurried. Two ran for signal flags, then positioned themselves in the lawn by hangar two. They jockeyed their flags with gusto. The airship cruised low and close, its motors droning a low musical accompaniment.

Ropes dropped in curls, forward and aft of the glassy gondola. A mix of pilots, mechanics, baggage handlers, and airline agents stared up. The appearance of dangling ropes triggered them to latch on. Shouting to each other joyously at the novelty, they dragged the airship to Horace's chosen parking spot, hand by hand, hauling it down out of the sky. Its engines cut. Its propellers beat to a standstill, and it settled silently to rest, the only sound a steady chugging from a gas compressor. From its gondola extended three widely splayed wheels, and the airship balanced on them nicely.

The small crowd gathered around, tittering in curious expectancy.

"It says Carroway Aeronautics by the fins! What's that?"

"Who's inside?"

"It's very streamlined."

The rear gondola door banged open, and a folding metal ladder tumbled out, thudding to the lawn. Two slim figures in flight suits nimbly whisked down the ladder, then stood at the foot, flanking the ladder. They kept a foot and a hand on the ladder to steady it, and possibly to keep the dirigible from floating away. They were very young, a boy and a girl, and they smiled broadly at the English welcome party.

With the ladder thus secured, a gangly man in cowboy boots and a Stetson hat climbed down. He carried a hammer and several long metal spikes. To the thrill of the crowd, he said, "Howdy, folks!" and touched his hat brim.

"Hoy! 'At's an American for sure!" someone crowed. There was scattered applause.

As Stetson Hat ambled toward the tail of the airship, another man lumbered down, wearing a tweed three-piece suit. The suit must have been tailored for him because he was built like a rugby center, all arms and shoulders and upper chest. He also carried stakes and a hammer, and when he reached the ground he waved his fistful of tools at the crowd. Red hair, a bushy red mustache, and wild red eyebrows gave him a rumpled country squire aspect. He said, "All right?" in a comfortable East London accent.

The crowd found no thrill in the ordinariness of the redhead's hello, but they did sense a certain kinship. He was clearly a fellow Englishman, at least. A pilot asked, "Where d'you hail from? Who's the captain?"

The bulky squire threw his arms out and up to indicate the airship. "Ladies an' gentlemen, we 'ave accomplished a commutation from New York with a stopover in St. John's, Newfoundland. Two and a half days in the air, ladies an' gentleman! This is the *Sky Arrow One*, an' this is 'er maiden voyage. She's a dream." He smiled beatifically.

The Stetson-wearing lanky man pounded in stakes and lashed the airship to the ground, rope by rope. He called over, "Gooper. They asked who the captain was, ya bull-necked buffoon. Also, stop shirkin' and start workin'!"

"Ow, put a sock in it, ya bowlegged saguaro!" Gooper bawled back, then beamed at the little crowd. "Pay 'im no mind. Tombstone is a few cards short of a full deck. The captain is none other than Ace Carroway, o' course! Excuse me. Pardon me. Coming through." The muscular man in tweed went to pound in his own set of stakes to secure the airship.

One by one, crowd members noticed another figure. No one had observed her slip down the ladder, but she stood among them now. She was trim of figure, dressed in a flight suit with a broad belt. Her deep gold skin, eyes, and tousled short hair were striking enough, and the four parallel scars angled down her temple and cheek added to the impression. But the most vivid aspect of the apparition could not easily be put into words. She seemed electric, with a vibrant presence and an intense awareness of the present moment. She was *alive*. And she was alive *now*.

"Thank you, Gilbert. Thank you, Vivian," she told the pair of grinning, flight-suited youths. She scanned the crowd. "Thank you for your help, one and all. I know it's a surprise to have an airship land. You handled it as if it happened every Tuesday."

"Ooo! I love that American accent!" said a young mechanic, his face coloring.

A pilot tapped a finger on his chin. "Ace Carroway. Now, why does that ring a bell?"

"She shortened the Great War is why," said a female voice speaking in Oxford accents. "She landed a top-secret Ottoman bomber-dirigible in Piccadilly Circus is why. A proud day."

The little crowd shifted to catch a look at the speaker. A woman in a leather jacket and scarf stood in a military at-ease posture, hands loosely clasped behind her. Wisps of gray-ripened blonde hair dangled in front of blue eyes that twinkled.

The scarred airship captain's gaze riveted to the middle-aged woman. An expression of wonder bloomed across Ace's face. "It can't be!"

"Hesitant though I am to contradict you…" Laugh marks at the corners of the woman's eyes deepened.

"Commander Harcourt! I can't believe it!"

Ace raced to the older woman and they embraced, laughing.

Chapter 5

Ace released Harcourt and held her at arm's length, grinning wide. The little crowd diffused, some strolling to ogle the airship, some returning to their various duties. Gooper pointedly cleared his throat.

Ace glanced back at the wide man and chuckled. "Time for introductions, I see. Joyce Harcourt, please meet Phileas Locknard. We usually call him Gooper."

The chesty gent with flame hair bowed. "Ma'am 'Arcourt!"

Harcourt blinked. "A pleasure. Gooper, was it?"

Ace chuckled. "The nickname might have something to do with the fact that he's a biologist. And this is Gregory Jamison. We call him Tombstone."

The skyscraper with the Stetson swept it off and bowed. "Ma'am."

"A pleasure, Tombstone. Are you from Arizona, perchance?"

"Texas, ma'am."

Ace grinned. "Understandable assumption, Commander. Gentleman, this is Joyce Harcourt, my Commander in the Ghost Squadron."

Ace gestured to the youths in spotless white flight suits. "These are Vivian and Gilbert, brother and sister. They crew the airship."

Gilbert grinned. "We didn't know we'd get to see England, though!"

Vivian chimed in. "We thought we were just training!"

Harcourt inclined her head. "A pleasure, Vivian and Gilbert."

Ace handed Vivian a scrap of paper, "Vivian? Could you please call the telegraph office for messages?" Vivian nodded and strode off to the control tower. She spun as she walked to drink in the exotic English ambiance and the foreign manners and clothes of the milling airport employees.

With the airship secured, a bouncy Ace pulled a willing Joyce Harcourt up into the gondola. Harcourt marveled at the clean, functional interior. The bridge faced forward. It merged without barriers to a lounge that occupied the middle of the gondola. Eight tiny cabins lined the back corridor.

Ace planted her fists on her hips. "*Sky Arrow One* was built to carry passengers. She's the prototype for a production airship."

"Production? There is a factory?" Harcourt said.

"Under construction, yes. In Lark Haven."

Tombstone drawled, "She's got a hard outer skin, an' the framing inside is duralumin. Two of the engines are set high up, 'way above center. That gives the pilot powered control over pitch in case you need the nose up or down."

"The real reason is so Ace can do loop-the-loops in 'er!" Gooper chuckled.

Ace protested, "I have no desire to do loop-the-loops in—" Ace broke off sheepishly. "Alright, you caught me. I do want to see if I can loop the *Sky Arrow*. But I can't do it this trip. You brought too many specimen bottles, Gooper! I don't want to break them and spill *smell* all over."

"Perish the thought." Gooper threw his massive chest out and his mustache drooped.

Ace glanced at Joyce Harcourt. "He's studying bio-luminescence."

Joyce blinked. "Bio-what?"

Tombstone said, "Some critters glow. Gooper's findin' out how."

Gooper nodded, his wilted mustache recovering. "I've isolated a goodly amount of luciferase now. Wot I'd like ter know is 'ow fireflies turn their lights *off*. Turnin' on is easy."

After the brief tour, Gilbert served tea in the lounge.

"Just one cup," Ace said, apologetically. "We're in a hurry. Sam has dug up a mystery, and we should go to the British Museum before it closes for the day."

"'E didn't dig it up!" chortled Gooper. "It screamed at 'im, more like."

"Sam?" inquired Harcourt.

Ace said, "Sam Raia Biming, one of my five associates at the agency and an archaeologist."

Harcourt raised her eyebrows. "Agency?"

Tombstone grinned. "C. Carroway an' Associates detective agency of New York, ma'am. We left Quack an' Bert mannin' the desk. Kinda like lettin' termites mind the wood house, I say."

Harcourt said, "Quack? Bert? Wait, never mind. I'm sure it's not relevant."

Ace pursed her lips at Tombstone. "The agency will be fine. Mrs. Figgins is there, remember?"

"She is. An' a good thing, too." Tombstone's long face drooped like a pessimistic mortician.

Harcourt tapped a finger on pursed lips. "May I

come with you to the Museum? I've retired from the RAF. I've got time."

Ace blinked, then smiled. "Why, that would be wonderful!"

"Is this regarding the affair at Stonehenge? Blood splattered everywhere and a death scream? I read about it. Most peculiar."

"Just so, Commander," Ace said.

"I'm just Joyce, now, and it feels rather nice." Harcourt sipped from her cup of tea, then almost spit it out in sudden agitation. "Oh! Your Sam must be the same Sam Biming mentioned in the *Times*! The archaeologist?"

Ace said, "Yes, that's him. He sent an interesting telegram as we were about to launch *Sky Arrow One's* maiden voyage. It caused us to change our destination."

Harcourt said, "You landed in London. Where was your original destination?"

"Hoboken, New Jersey!" Tombstone chuckled. "We ended up goin' a hundred times farther."

"Plans are made to be scrapped and rewritten," Ace said placidly.

Harcourt's brows knitted. "You crossed the Atlantic Ocean *on a whim*?"

Vivian returned. She approached Ace with a scrap of paper held out. "It's from Dr. Biming, Ace."

Ace read out loud. "Plot thickens. Helm of Amun stolen from British Museum and replaced by gold ankh representing Nephthys, goddess of death."

"Helm of what? Neff-thiss who?" Tombstone said, raising his hat and rubbing a wrinkled forehead.

Ace leapt to her feet. "We need to get to the Museum. *Now.*"

The quartet caught a cab to the British Museum. The youthful Gilbert and Vivian stayed in Croydon to look after the airship.

In the jostling cab, Joyce Harcourt studied Ace's profile and the prominent diagonal white scars marking her dark skin. "Are those scars from your crash landing in the Himalayas, Ace?"

Ace glanced across at Harcourt. "Related to it."

"Well, I hope you've got nine lives, like a cat, because you've used up two of them. That Himalaya crash was the second time I wrote you off as dead. The first was on the French front, of course."

"I'm sure I've got one life, like everybody else."

"I'm glad you're alive, Ace."

"Likewise, Commander."

"Joyce."

"I'll try … Joyce. But you'll always be my commander."

"Ha! I don't deserve it. But just to confuse you more, I made Air Commodore before I retired."

"Air Commodore Harcourt. It has a nice ring to it."

"So does Joyce."

Ace grinned.

The cab wound through London streets until it rattled to a stop in front of the British Museum. Ace attempted to foist American coins on the cabbie, but he squinted dubiously at the odd-looking currency. A laughing Harcourt settled the bill.

Tombstone unfolded his lanky frame from the cab, stretched, and replaced his Stetson on his head. Before him ascended stately marble columns supporting a gently triangular roofline. Lined up on the high façade, classical Greek sculptures posed. Far below, broad marble steps that marched with geometrical perfection. Tombstone whistled appreciation of its grandeur, then squinted sourly. "British Museum? That ain't British. It's Greek. I'd bet mah horse on it."

Gooper scowled. "Oi don't want yer 'orse, mate."

"Good, b'cause Sparky don't like you."

"Wot? Oi've never met yer 'orse!"

"Yeah, well, when you do, he won't like you."

Ace said, "Fellas. Walk faster. Talk less."

At the information desk, the neat, cheery fellow behind the counter blinked up at Ace. She said, "We'd like to see Sam Biming, please. He'll be halfway expecting us."

The fellow's smile faded and he nibbled his own lower lip. Leaning forward, he said, "Begging your pardon, ladies and gentlemen, but I'm to direct all such inquiries to Museum Security. Through that door just there."

"Eh, wot?" Gooper grumbled.

After exchanging puzzled glances, they all trooped through the door marked "Security."

A man in a tweed suit loitered near. A clean-cut gentleman on the young side of thirty, he seemed one of the many scholars that daily flooded the museum. After the Carroway party disappeared into the security room, he sauntered over to one side of the doorway and began to pack tobacco into a pipe.

The Carroway party presented themselves to a graying woman in a navy blue uniform. "We'd like to see Sam Biming, please," Ace repeated.

No swift answer came. The uniformed woman first requested their names, addresses, and whereabouts for the last week. After jotting notes about New York and airships, she opened up. "Sorry. Sorry about that. It's just that Sam Biming went missing. He didn't come to the Museum this morning, and the police say he didn't sleep at his flat last night."

"What?" Tombstone said, worriedly.

"Oh, dear," put in Joyce Harcourt.

Ace all but vibrated with tightly bottled energy. "Go on. What else can you tell us? We came all the way from America to help with the mystery he'd found."

"Yes, ma'am. I suppose I can say that there was a theft here at the museum. Yesterday or the day before. Dr. Biming discovered it. We're all a bit on edge. Sorry. Also, we haven't told the press, yet. We were hoping it was a mistake. You know, a clerical error. An item swapped out for cleaning but not written down. That sort of thing."

"But it wasn't a mistake, I take it? What was stolen?"

"Ah, something from Egypt. Let me see." The guard shuffled papers on her desk while her four visitors exchanged glances of worry. "Ah, here. It's the Helm of Amun, whatever that is. Oh, right, and we were gifted as well. I forgot that. Someone left a gold ankh. And, before you ask, we don't have it. The police took it for evidence."

Joyce Harcourt frowned. "Are there not any clues

at all? For the whereabouts of Sam Biming, I mean."

The uniformed woman sighed. "Ask Scotland Yard. I haven't heard anything. I think we're going to have the newspapers over after the Museum closes. Again, so sorry for the red tape. Orders. Unofficially, you're cleared, naturally. You were en route at the time of the disappearance."

"I suppose we'll head straight for Scotland Yard." Ace's mouth formed a grim straight line.

The man in tweed finished packing his pipe and sauntered well away before the party left the security office.

A Londoner might scratch their head if asked the location of the Metropolitan Police Service. If asked about Scotland Yard, they would immediately give directions. The two were one and the same, of course, but the unofficial nickname vastly overshadowed its official counterpart.

The Carroway party spoke to a detective, but they learned nothing more about Sam. They did get to view all three of the solid gold ankhs, laid out side by side. They gleamed seductively. One collected from Stonehenge, one from the house of a Devonshire heiress, and one from the British Museum.

"Horus, Isis, and Nephthys. They are casts, but molded from sculptures by the same hand," Ace murmured.

The hovering detective raised an eyebrow. "A bit

spooky to hear you say that, ma'am. That's exactly how our appraiser put it. Can you shed any light on this affair?"

Ace spread her hands. "Sam would be the one to ask. My own knowledge is very incomplete. All I can tell you is that these are in an ancient style typical of Thebes, that is, the Upper Nile region. In that pantheon, the most important god was Amun, the hidden god. No images of Amun are made, but sometimes there is a blank space to represent his presence. Isis and Nephthys are sisters who symbolically represent life and death, respectively. Horus, with the falcon head, is Isis's son, a heroic figure sympathetic to the plight of mortals. Such sympathy is not common amongst ancient Egyptian gods.

"That gold appears to be very pure, though I'm sure your appraiser will have measured its density, so you'll have the exact number. From the lack of dents and scuffs, I would guess these ankhs were cast recently. They seem fresh from polishing at the hands of the sculptor. Alternatively, they could have been sitting untouched in a tomb for millennia — but unhandled during that time."

The detective listened, slack-jawed. Joyce Harcourt smiled in fond reminiscence. Gooper's mustache fluffed in amusement. "Ask a simple question, eh? But I don't suppose even Ace knows what it means. Two thefts and a midnight scream with blood."

Ace exhaled, inflating her cheeks. "I have no clue what it means! It is utterly baffling." Ace narrowed eyes at the detective. "And not a clue about Sam's disappearance? He just … vanished?"

The detective nodded soberly. "Not a trace."

34

Chapter 6

The four hurried back to the British Museum to try to catch the press conference. As they trotted along, Joyce Harcourt saw Gooper glance at her feet. She had seen old-fashioned gentlemen make similar solicitous glances before. She winked at Gooper. "Perhaps I should mention that I walk a fair bit. And I gave up impractical shoes several decades ago."

Gooper straightened up. His mustache twitched. He mumbled, "Oh, aye, ma'am. Absolutely, ma'am."

In the next instant, his boot toe caught on a cobblestone. "Ow!" He staggered forward.

Tombstone grew a big grin.

Ace covered her mouth as if concealing a burp.

Harcourt tossed in a diplomatic distraction. "Oh, look. There's the Museum, just ahead."

They arrived a little late. The meeting room contained several reporters scribbling on pads and a pair of worried museum officials mournfully giving out facts. Sound echoed inside the marble museum walls, amplifying voices and pencil scratches.

Ace drifted to the dimmest corner of the room and slouched there as inconspicuous as she could make her tall, scarred, flight-suited self. After a minute, Gooper and Tombstone guessed the reason for her uncharacteristic reticence. They drifted toward her corner and positioned themselves between the reporters and Ace. Their odd and lumpy screen may or may not have been effective, but in any case, the famed flyer was not accosted by the newshawks.

As the four listened, they learned that the display case lock was broken. One curator held up a sketch of the Helm of Amun, a flat-topped Egyptian crown set with gems. The other described the ankh of Nephthys. The reporters asked questions, but most of the answers were simply, "I'm afraid we don't know."

The reporters flipped closed their notebooks, and the meeting broke up.

"Excellent burglary, if you can call burglary excellent," Harcourt remarked. She then trotted to catch up to one of the two museum officials. "Oh, sir! Might I see the display case?"

The fellow wore a tweed suit, the apparent unofficial uniform at the British Museum. He peered through owlish spectacles at Harcourt. "Yes, I suppose, madam. You realize it is empty?"

"Yes, of course, but nevertheless?" Harcourt smiled at the older gentleman. He mumbled a bemused assent and gestured for her to carry on.

Gooper lumbered after Harcourt and Tombstone ambled bowlegged in the rear. Ace, however, was arrested by a voice behind her. "Pardon, Miss. A word, if you please?"

Ace pivoted in sharp alarm, but the tall man who spoke held no pencil or reporter's notebook. Dapper in museum-standard tweed, a stem of a pipe peeked out of his jacket pocket. He lifted his cap in polite greeting. He seemed an outdoors type. He possessed appealing crow's feet at the corners of his light gray eyes, long dimples in his cheek, and a tan deeper than England alone could explain.

At the absence of a press badge, Ace relaxed. "Yes?"

"Ah, yes! Oh, my!" Suddenly eye to eye with Ace, the fellow wrung his hands together and stared. He seemed to lose the power of speech, and color rose from his neck to his cheeks.

Ace watched the performance in perplexity. "Is there something I can help you with?"

The man whipped his hands behind his back and stammered, "A-allow me to introduce myself. I am Darby Entwhistle, assistant to the archaeologist Miles Fairweather."

Ace glanced left, then right, but the reporters had gone. "Cecilia Carroway."

The handsome, very British fellow smelled faintly of pipe smoke. "Cecilia Carroway. What a lovely name. I mean, sorry. Sorry, I mean a pleasure. A great pleasure."

Ace's eyes widened. She stopped her hand from rising to touch her facial scars. "And how can I help you, Mr. Entwhistle?"

"Mm?" Entwhistle gazed at Ace with a vacant smile on his face. "Oh! It's about your friend. I assume he is your friend. Dr. Biming, I mean."

"What about Sam?"

"Ah, he is a friend. I'm glad my guess is correct. Allow me to explain. I'm attached to the Miles Fairweather expedition, shortly bound for Thebes, Egypt. In light of this awful theft business, perhaps a destination of keen interest, eh? Thebes is written all over it. Sorry, I'm off track. What I mean is, if you should be footloose, Miss Carroway, I mean, what I mean is, it would be perfectly smashing if you were to join up!" Darby's stumbling tongue came to the point at last.

Ace's brow furrowed. "You're inviting me to come

to Thebes? On an archaeological expedition?"

Entwhistle tugged at his collar with a finger to loosen it. "Yes, quite. Just so, just so." A new tinge of pink flushed his tanned face.

Ace said coolly, "Well, it's nice to know I'm invited, but I don't think it will be possible."

"Oh, of course, of course! I know I sound half-mad and probably fresh as a daisy. I do apologize. I do think, however …" Darby leaned closer and lowered his voice. "I do think that the mystery of the missing Dr. Biming might be cleared up by coming with the Fairweather expedition. Yes, I'm sure of it."

Ace narrowed her eyes. "That's an odd thing to say! How could it be cleared up?"

"Well, now. There are reasons! Dr. Fairweather and Dr. Biming are colleagues, for one. And Thebes, the source of the iconography on the ankhs. If the riddle is to be solved, it is at Thebes." Darby spoke earnestly and imploringly.

"But Sam Biming disappeared in London. Thebes must be three thousand miles from here."

"Yes, yes. True, so true. I do not mean to say that Dr. Biming is in Thebes, merely that the ankhs come from there. I do hope he turns up. I'd hate to think any harm has come to such a respected scholar."

"He'd *better* turn up," Ace grumbled.

"Oh, would you consider joining the expedition, Miss Carroway? *Would* you?"

"My answer stands," Ace said firmly.

"Yes, yes, of course, of course. Ah, but Miss Carroway, do ring me up at the Beaumont if you change your mind. The Beaumont Hotel. Well, if you change your mind quickly, I mean. I'll be leaving to join Dr.

Fairweather the day after tomorrow. He left a bit early to squeeze in a little vacation in the south of France."

"Of course. Goodbye to you, Mr. Entwhistle." Ace inclined her head, then padded off with characteristic swiftness into the marble chambers of the museum.

Entwhistle's voice followed her. "Until then, Miss Carroway! A pleasure! Farewell! Farewell!"

Chapter 7

Dinner conversation was full of worried silences, and none of the four felt sleepy afterward. Late hour notwithstanding, they strolled out to wander the London streets. In unspoken accord, they drifted toward quieter streets, ending somewhere in Covent Gardens near the banks of the Thames.

Joyce Harcourt said, for the third time, "I certainly hope that Sam is all right."

"Boy, howdy, you can say that again. I'm missin' that li'l shorty somethin' awful," Tombstone agreed.

The fog rolled in for the night again. The moist air turned clammy and soon the street lamps dimmed. Shadows ruled the London streets.

Harcourt shivered and heaved a sigh. "Well, this has been lovely, but I suppose I'll be heading home. Gooper. Tombstone. Such a pleasure to meet— What was that?"

A soft bleat, common on a farm but startling and alien in central London, emerged above the continuous rumbling of distant trains and trucks.

The party froze, straining their ears, each facing a different direction. Ace whispered, "It sounded like an animal. The snort of a piglet? If I'm backtracking the echoes correctly, it came from up there." The pilot pointed forward and left.

In unspoken agreement, they all stopped talking and tiptoed in the direction Ace indicated. A block later, they drifted into a deserted cobblestone street and slowed. The sound had not repeated. The fog-filled space across the street sounded like empty space to the ear, except for the swish and gurgle of water. They had arrived at the banks of the River Thames, it seemed.

As they milled in uncertainty on the cobblestones, it jaggedly cut the air: a horrific scream, sudden and un-nerving. The ragged, raw, primal shriek seemed ripped from the throat of one caught in the unexpected agony of onrushing death.

All four were war veterans intimately acquainted with danger. Still, this deathly screech blanched each face and locked every muscle in their bodies.

Joyce Harcourt recovered first. "That sounded less than cheery," she muttered with impeccable British understatement.

"Come on!" Ace flung an arm out in the direction from which the agonized cry had come.

They ran across cobblestones, hearts hammering. When the plaza beyond emerged from the fog, all four stopped as if hitting an invisible wall. The paved floor of the plaza glistened with lanes of blood, all radiating from a central spot. The most distant of the crimson rays splashed upon the base of a stone obelisk that loomed tall in the ghostly fog. Nothing moved except for the slow glistening and oozing of the blood.

Open-mouthed, they tiptoed closer. The asterisk of blood spatter only grew more horrific. The four-sided obelisk emerged more clearly from the fog, its surface crowded with Egyptian hieroglyphs. Beyond the base of the stone spire loomed a featureless gloom, and the sounds of swishing waters grew. A low stone parapet marked the bank edge, past which flowed the Thames.

To the right of the obelisk, at the river's edge, a

shadow moved.

Ace sprinted toward it. Its vaguely teardrop outline sank out of sight.

Belatedly, the others scrambled to follow. Ace paused at the parapet and crouched as if getting ready to leap into the river.

As the group arrived, Ace slowly straightened up, arms dropping to her side. She emitted a sound: a warbling hum, otherworldly and ethereal. Its pleasant melody contrasted with the gory backdrop of the blood-striped plaza behind her.

Gooper glanced at her, then followed her eyes outward to the sluggish, fog-enfolded river. "Wot's out there, Ace?"

"I could have sworn that Horus himself spied on us. I saw the falcon beak and the peaked crown." Ace spun to stare at her companions.

A nervous smile flitted across Harcourt's face. "I'm glad you said that. I saw the beak, too — and doubted my own sanity."

Tombstone leaned over the parapet to examine the vertical stone wall that dropped into the river. "Horus, huh? Wull, where'd the feller go? Turned invisible?"

Ace tugged at her lower lip. "On the water, I saw what might have been a canoe. But it moved much faster than I can swim. In moments, it disappeared into the fog."

Ace's eyes drifted toward the grisly splashes of crimson. "Gooper, how long would it take you to cook up an Uhlenhuth test on this blood? And, speaking of that, please sacrifice a handkerchief in the name of science and soak up as much blood as you can."

Gooper nodded and patted himself down.

"What th' heck's an Oolen-hooth test?" Tombstone muttered.

Harcourt emitted a shaky laugh. "I'm glad you said that, Tombstone. I hate to always be the ignorant one in the crowd."

Gooper tugged a nose rag out of his pocket, then a pocket knife. He dug deeper. Next, he extracted a few coins, a pencil stub, a length of string, and a miniature leaf press. Finally, he cooed, "Ah, 'ere she is! An eyedropper. An' as fer the Uhlenhuth test, that'd be Paul Uhlenhuth, an 'is invention of a way to tell a species from their blood. Wot Ace is gettin' at is that this 'ere blood may be 'uman, and it may *not* be 'uman. And no bloke can't tell by lookin'. You need th' Uhlenhuth test. As fer 'ow long, that's simple. I can't do it. I mean, I *could*, but I'd need enzymes from a university or Scotland Yard or summat."

Gooper hunched over to draw some of the blood up into his eyedropper. Joyce Harcourt's eyes tracked along the lanes of blood spatter. She pointed toward the center of the rays of blood. "What's that over there? I see gold."

Ace stepped past Gooper and tiptoed to the spot. Seconds later, a small gleaming bit of metal dangled from her hand. "It's another ankh!"

Ace gazed at it, turning it this way and that in her hand. "The ankh is similar to the other three. Solid gold, surely. It is not covered in blood, so it was probably placed after the bloodletting. The carving, or mold, is of Seth, brother to Isis and Nephthys. Those three gods have but one remaining sibling, and his name is Osiris."

"Well, at least there is some semblance of a pattern," Joyce Harcourt wrung her hands.

"One more thing," Tombstone said. He stood bowlegged, thumbs hooked into his belt, frowning at the blood.

Gooper stored his eyedropper inside his leaf press and raised bushy eyebrows to peer suspiciously at Tombstone. "Wot, cowboy?"

"These here splashes. They come from outside in, not inside out. The way the li'l drops are, see? The li'l tadpole tails point out."

Gooper whipped his head down to view the blood. "Leather beanpole has sharp eyes."

Harcourt's brow wrinkled. "So, even though it looks like something bloody exploded in the center, that's not what happened?"

Tombstone's face mourned. "No, ma'am. These stripes were more like painted on. Or, mebbe more accurate, thrown down."

Ace chewed her lower lip. "There are exactly twenty-four stripes. It reminds me that our twenty-four-hour day is inherited from ancient Egyptian astronomers."

Harcourt waved a hand at the obelisk standing silently over them. "Like this. They call this Cleopatra's Needle. It's stood here ever since I can remember."

Ace blew air into her cheeks. Her gaze flitted to the obelisk and its carved hieroglyphics. "Oh, yes. Everything's screaming ancient Egypt. That's for sure."

She glanced at the trinket dangling from her fingers. "These are all very specific clues, but I don't know how to read them! And it doesn't get us any closer to finding Sam."

Chapter 8

A full day later, they were no nearer finding Sam. Scotland Yard inspected the blood-splashed obelisk. They accepted Gooper's blood sample and the Ankh of Seth and promised to share the results. The rest of their time disappeared into fruitless library research and a good deal of pacing and rumination. Joyce Harcourt joined them for supper, and they talked things over.

Ace sighed. "In summary, we are stymied. Out of sheer desperation, I propose joining the Fairweather expedition."

"The Fairweather expedition? What, now?" Joyce Harcourt asked bemusedly, smoothing back a lock of brown hair with a few gray strands in it.

Ace explained about Darby Entwhistle and Miles Fairweather heading to Thebes, ending with, "What keeps coming back to my mind is how certain this Entwhistle was that we would solve Sam's whereabouts. The word he used was *iconography* as if Egyptian hieroglyphs were going to tell us where Sam was."

Tombstone paused in working a toothpick through his teeth and squinted at Ace. "Who'd this feller invite, exactly? All of us or jes' you?"

Ace blinked. "Just me, I guess."

Gooper harrumphed. "'E sounds like a bloke chasin' skirt, t' me. Liable ter say anything."

Ace sent Gooper a quelling glance, then said to Joyce, "Ma'am? Are you free for some piloting? If you want an adventure, you could join Vivian and Gilbert in the *Sky Arrow* and shadow the rest of us as we go to Thebes with Fairweather and Entwhistle."

Joyce's eyes gradually widened. "Fly an airship? Me? Why, why, why, I'd be delighted!"

"It's not an imposition?" Ace smiled.

"Absolutely not! I can have Bess look after the plants and bring the mail in. Don't change your mind now! I want to! When do we leave?"

"I understood Entwhistle to say he was leaving to-morrow, but the *Sky Arrow* will be faster than whatever he's got. So, you can have days, if you want them. The important thing is to make sure you understand our tracking gear. I have a pulse transmitter. It looks like a suitcase, but on the inside it's a long-range radio that sends out a ping every ten seconds. You'll be able to track us from the *Sky Arrow* using its loop receiver. If we are going to Thebes, we'll have to pass through Cairo. You can pick us up there and shadow us there-after, comfortably beyond the horizon. I can key the pulses too, so I can send Morse code if we have some-thing to say."

"Very fancy!"

Ace laid a finger beside her nose. "Let's see. Any-thing else? Dress both for the desert and a high alti-tude flight. And, if you have a gun, bring it. I trust Entwhistle about as far as I can throw Gooper."

Gooper flexed his bulging arms like a circus strongman.

Tombstone slapped a palm against his own fore-head in mock despair.

"You fellas don't mind being chaperones, do you? To poor, helpless me?" Ace attempted to flutter her eyelashes with limited success.

"Cor! 'Elpless!" Gooper snorted.

"Chaperonin' Ace? That's like a horny toad teachin' a 'gator how to bite."

Darby Entwhistle lugged his heavy suitcase through the lobby of the Beaumont Hotel. He passed a fluted marble column, then almost collided with the next stationary object: a quiet, tall figure dressed in a flight suit with a wide belt.

"Oh!" he exclaimed. "Oh, I say!"

"Surprise," Ace said dryly. "I hope it's not too much of a shock, but I'd like to come with you to Thebes after all. What ship and when?"

Darby bounced up and down. Breathlessly, he replied, "Oh, smashing! Positively brilliant! I'm beside myself, truly! You are coming along, coming with us to Kush! I mean, Thebes. You will grace the journey most admirably." His eyelids blinked several times, and he amended, "I mean, your contribution to the expedition will be truly inestimable, and we are honored to be graced by your presence!"

"What," Ace said at about the same speed and temperature as an alpine glacier, "ship and when?"

"Oh! Oh, pardon. Pardon me. A thousand pardons. It is the *Teatime* actually. At Tilbury docks. Confusing name, what? The *Teatime* does a Channel crossing at four in the afternoon, hence the name *Teatime*, I presume, ha ha! Oh, sorry. Sorry, I'm all giddy. Positively giddy. Yes, four in the afternoon on the *Teatime*. It will take some time to unload when we get to France. Big crates, you see. Big ones." Darby gestured with his hands to illustrate how very large the big crates were.

"We'll be there. Ta-ta!" Ace said, then turned on her heel and marched out at a brisk speed.

"Ta-ta! Ta-ta! Very British of you. Pip pip and all that, what? And we'll see—" Darby broke off. He regrouped. "Wait. 'We?' 'We'll' be there? 'We,' who? I mean, who is 'we?'" But Ace was gone.

Chapter 9

The small steamer announced itself in bold letters at both stern and bow, "TEATIME." Darby Entwhistle was already aboard when Ace, Gooper, and Tombstone climbed up the gangplank with their luggage. His greetings were polite and gracious. Although he said no disagreeable word, he showed none of the exuberance he gushed when he thought it would be Ace by herself.

Ace, Tombstone, and Gooper each carried two suitcases. One of each pair contained clothes and kit. Ace's spare suitcase held a portable radio transmitter, Gooper's a biochemical laboratory, and Tombstone's a trove of vacuum tubes, resistors, capacitors, inductors, wires, pan-pots, and other electrical gear.

The clement streak of weather improved even more, and they were treated to a sunset with only a few clouds as they made the crossing to Calais, France. The *Teatime* was half ferry and half cargo steamer. There were no passenger cabins, but a spartan lounge held benches and some tables. A ring of windows preserved the scenery but screened out the breeze. A dozen passengers whiled away the time inside as the chugging engines pushed the *Teatime* through choppy waters.

Ace had abandoned her flight suit for knickers and a sweater that hung almost to her knees. Leaning against a window, she glanced for a moment at Entwhistle, then back to the clouds and whitecaps. "Tell me about the Fairweather expedition," she said.

Benched next to her, Darby Entwhistle half-closed his eyes and rattled off a reply. "The site Miles has found is somewhat south of the first cataract. That is, south of Aswan, which was called Swenett in antiquity. The temples at Thebes and Luxor have a similar artistic style, so it's sort of a Luxor-south sort of place."

"What's a cataract?" Tombstone sat near, shuffling a deck of playing cards.

"Waterfall." Gooper sat across the table from Tombstone.

Tombstone squinted at Gooper. "The Nile's got waterfalls?"

Darby glanced at the pair. "Yes, indeed, numbered from north to south. Well, the first cataract is no more. There is a dam there now. It has navigation locks, so ships can pass farther upstream than they could in ancient Egypt."

Ace said, "Upstream of Aswan would lie outside the boundaries of the Old Kingdoms of Egypt, yes? The first cataract was the so-called opening of Egypt. So, we'll be in Nubia."

Darby nodded like a sage. "Well, that is the question, isn't it? Maybe the ruins are Nubian, and maybe we've got the history wrong, and Egypt was once bigger than we thought! Enter Miles Fairweather, the famous Egyptologist." Darby gestured in theatrical introduction though no Dr. Fairweather appeared. "I'm sure he'll find a way to answer that question along with many others. We'll catch up to him at Genoa. Then, we'll take a freighter to Cairo."

"What's your role in this expedition, pardner?" Tombstone drawled.

"Logistics, sir!" Darby said brightly, touching the rim of his tweed cap. "Miles needs all sorts of things, from soft brushes to coffee grounds to, well, you name it. Did I explain what is next? We'll sleep in Calais whilst our shipping crates are loaded on a train. Then, it's a relaxing day and night aboard the train to Genoa. I arranged that and things like that. Busy, busy. Lists and more lists."

The faint odor of pipe tobacco emanated from Entwhistle's tweed coat. His tall but spare frame buzzed with energy as he spoke. His gray eyes rested most frequently on Ace's face.

Ace faced Entwhistle squarely. "And what's your theory on what happened to Sam? Even now, I'm not sure I should be here. I could simply stay on the *Teatime* and return to London. Convince me."

Darby nodded gravely. "I can oblige, Miss Carroway. We're not in a crowd of reporters, now, so I can speak freely. The connection is those ankhs. I know *exactly* where they come from, and it's the site Miles Fairweather has found."

Ace's eyebrows raised. "You're certain?"

"Absolutely. They are unique. I don't know how they got to England, or why they were being dropped here and there. It all seems preposterous. I don't know where Sam Biming is, but I do wonder if I know where he's going."

Ace said, "You're going to say Fairweather's dig, aren't you?" Tombstone and Gooper stayed quiet, listening. Tombstone dealt cards.

Darby smiled wistfully at Ace. "You read my mind. But check my logic. From what I read in the papers, no one has *died*. I mean, there are no bodies. Those bloodthirsty reporters *want* there to be bodies, but there aren't any. Suppose Dr. Biming isn't a victim at all. It's equally plausible that he is on the hunt. He is hot on the trail of this mystery, and he simply hasn't had time to tell anyone where he went."

Ace fell silent. The gold flecks in her irises seemed to spiral as she stared into space.

Gooper picked up his cards and fanned them out. "Got any fives, mate?"

Tombstone said, "Go fish."

Ace said, "All right. I'm still in. To Nubia we go."

The hotel in Calais was happy to accommodate extra paying guests. Darby Entwhistle begged off dinner and disappeared.

A subdued Gooper toiled over a crème brûlée dessert too petite to handle with his ham hands. "Yew sure we're chasin' the right rabbit, Ace?"

"I'm not sure about anything. But even if we are on the wrong trail, Scotland Yard has a better chance of finding Sam than we do. They have hundreds more feet and eyes." Ace poked a spoon into her own dessert but ate none.

"I think this character Darby's up to somethin', anyways." Tombstone had already eaten every scrap of food in front of him.

"What have you noticed?" Ace asked.

Tombstone drawled, "Wull, what kinda archaeologist takes a vacation an' lets his assistant arrange everything? I mean, mebbe that's how a big game hunter would do it, but it don't ring true fer a serious scholarly endeavor."

"I 'ates to agree wif you, Tombstone, but you've 'it the nail on the 'ead wif that one!" Gooper smiled, and his bushy red mustache smiled with him. The peaceful accord lasted only moments. Gooper let his mustache droop and whispered, "Lizard man!"

"Neanderthal!"

Ace chuckled in spite of herself. "Shush, you two. There's one more thing I noticed. Early this morning at the hotel, Darby let slip a new word. He said, 'Kush. I mean Thebes.' Kush is the ancient name for Nubia, a whole ancient kingdom, not a single site like Thebes, and also quite far away geographically. It struck me as odd."

There were nods of agreement, then Gooper raised a meaty finger. "I got one. Darby. He never relaxes. Even when nothing's 'appening, 'e's all rigid, like a king at court wif all eyes on him."

Tombstone jetted a puff of dismissive air from his nose. "He's a Brit. It's his nature to be stiff."

Ace smirked. "You might have a point, Gooper. Suppose you're right. What do you think has him tense?"

Gooper slowly rolled his bulky shoulders and pursed his lips, which in turn fluffed up his flaming red mustache. "Well, I think it's us. So I think 'e's hiding summat."

Ace's lips curled in a humorless smile. "Fair enough. We've a few thousand miles to travel before we will arrive somewhere south of Aswan. We can make a hobby of needling Mr. Entwhistle for more information. It might take a lot of patience. Are you still in?"

Tombstone laughed. "O' course, Ace! Say, if you're not gonna eat that there li'l sweet treat …"

Gooper's eyes suddenly widened. In dreamy tones, he said, "Cor! I might see a tora hartebeest!"

Tombstone ponderously wagged his head from side to side. "I ain't gonna ask."

Chapter 10

The Limited from Calais clacked and rumbled south through the French countryside. Ace, Gooper, and Tombstone gazed wistfully out the windows and pointed out hazily-remembered landmarks from their tours of duty during the Great War. Mid-morning, Ace conferred with the dining-car porter. Between them, they slid a table to one side, and Ace commenced her daily exercise regimen.

Darby Entwhistle entered the dining car from forward and smoothed the lapels of his tweed jacket. Confronted by the sight of a pair of trouser legs and bare feet poking into the air above table level at the far end of the car, his footsteps faltered. A perplexed line appeared between his eyebrows. The legs sinuously entwined, then fell into a cartwheel. Up spun Cecilia Carroway's tousled gold cropped head.

Darby gasped, and a smile lit his face.

Arms whipped around. Legs flew up in a scissor kick. The lithe tawny form dived for the car floor and disappeared entirely below tabletop level. "Amazing!" murmured Darby to himself.

"Y'all walkin' or jes' gawkin'?" said a voice in Darby's ear.

He spun around with a start to find himself staring at a chest. The shirt hanging on that spare frame showed Western styling in its snaps and pockets, framed in a leather vest. Above the collar, the dour and unshaven visage of Tombstone squinted down in distaste.

"I say!" Darby Entwhistle blurted. "You gave me a start."

"Yup. 'Pparently so," the leathery cowboy drawled.

"Look. That's a bit rude, old chap." Entwhistle's face colored under his tan.

Tombstone shrugged his lean shoulders. "Yep. Good thing it ain't my job to be all saccharine-sweet like them poor porters."

"Why are you here, anyway? Since we're being all straightforwardly American and all, I'll just get this off my chest, shall I? As I recall it, I invited Miss Carroway and only her. You and your *wide* friend invited yourselves." His words vibrated with annoyance laced with a spritz of venom.

Tombstone's beetled eyebrows relaxed. He hooked thumbs in his tooled leather belt. "Glad fer some plain talk, Entwhistle. Mind iffen I call you Darby?"

"What? No, I suppose not."

"Darby, this is about Sam. Period. We're buddies since the Great War. That li'l shorty'd take a bullet fer me, and I'd take one fer him. I kin barely sleep a'night fer all the worryin' I'm doin'. There. That answer yer question?"

Entwhistle blinked. "Why, yes." He glanced over his shoulder. Ace was visible again, hands pressed palm to palm, eyes closed, standing on one leg with the other bent to place a foot on a knee. Darby regarded Tombstone once again. "So you and she …"

Tombstone scowled deeply. "Pardner, you want to court yonder Miss Carroway, go right ahead. You kin try diggin' to China with a toothpick, too. That'd be more productive."

"I, I see." Enwhistle's eyes wandered uncertainly about the dining car.

"Buddy, mebbe you ain't such a bad sort. I'll cut you a li'l slack. Here, I'll show you a game."

Darby snapped alarmed eyes back to the lanky cowpoke. "A game?"

Tombstone's cadaverous face cracked into a grin. "Yep. Do this." Tombstone raised his eyes to Ace and drawled, "April the first, year nine hundred ninety-nine A. D."

He hadn't raised his voice beyond a conversational level, and the dining car echoed with the rattles and bangs of rail travel. It seemed as if the woman at the other end of the car could barely have heard Tombstone. Nevertheless, without breaking her meditative pose, she called back, "Saturday."

Slowly, realization stole over Darby's face. His mouth dropped open. He pleaded to Tombstone, "Tell me she didn't just do that."

"Try it yourself, pardner."

The tweed-coated Brit was promptly rendered speechless.

Tombstone heaved a sigh. "May the fifteenth, nineteen hundred an' two."

"Thursday," came the placid alto answer.

"She ain't wrong. A few times, we checked up on her. Say, Darby?"

"Amazing. Stupendous. I'm flabbergasted. Eh, yes? What is it?"

"Kin you git outta my way? Been trying to squeeze past you fer ten minutes, now."

Farmland became pastures became foothills, and the sun's last rays shone in the right-side train windows as the Limited climbed into the Alps that separated France from Italy. The porters cleared away dinner and Tombstone dealt out his deck for a game of hearts. "Watch out fer the queen of spades. She's worth thirteen points you don't want. We call her Calamity Jane."

"Can I have that nickname?" Ace tapped the side of her nose.

Gooper's mustache twitched. "Too late for that, me bellwether compatriot. Too late by far."

Wedged between Gooper's bulging bicep and the window, Darby Entwhistle gazed across the table at Ace. "Amazing display of acrobatics today, Miss Carroway."

"Thank you," she answered curtly.

Darby's lips curved upward. "It reminds me of the *kekewe-saew*."

Ace perked up. "*Kekewe-saew?*"

Tombstone winced. "Don't give Gooper new words! What's that, now? Kay kay way sow?"

"Close," Darby nodded to Tombstone. "The *kekewe-saew* are the shadow-dancers to the pharaoh, renowned for their strength and flexibility."

"Dancers, huh?" Tombstone said.

"Yes. They entertain the pharaoh at court, performing dances and acrobatics for his pleasure."

"Wot's shadowy about 'em?" Gooper said.

"They are a closed and secret caste, for one," Darby replied with a storyteller's sinister relish. "But the secrecy is necessary: the *kekewe-saew* are a class of assassins."

"Assassins." Ace elevated her eyebrows.

"Oh, yes." Darby's voice hushed, and he bobbed his head to each of them with a conspiratorial wink. "To curry the disfavor of the pharaoh is doubly dangerous. Not only is the pharaoh's word law, but if the pharaoh is weary of speaking, he can send the *kekewe-saew* to eliminate any whose words cause dissension."

"I've never heard of them," Ace said flatly.

"Naturally not." Darby waved his fingers in an airy, dismissive circle.

An irresistible force pressed Darby on the shoulder and squeezed him against the window like a bug under glass. The tweed-jacketed Englishman peered over and down to see Gooper pressing a thick index finger into his shoulder, a finger as unstoppable as a freight train. Gooper's mustache bristled disapprovingly.

"Guv'," the red-haired Cockney said, each word deliberate. "Miss Carroway, 'ere, she's wot yew might call well-read. If she hain't heard of summat, then summat hain't in the lexicon."

Darby lifted his chin. "There is no need for that! I know they've never been heard of. Indeed, it's impossible that Miss Carroway, or any of you, had heard of the *kekewe-saew*."

"Why's that?" Tombstone said.

"Because it's a secret known only to Miles Fairweather and myself. Let me put it this way. Doctor Fairweather is already a famous archaeologist, but what he's discovering now makes all his previous work look like one stone from a whole pyramid."

62

Chapter II

As dawn lit broken parades of clouds in the upper airs, the Limited arrived in the bustling port of Genoa. Darby Entwhistle excused himself at the train station. "I need to hire some strong backs to get the crates aboard ship. It's the *Neptune* in case I didn't mention it. I'll meet you there as soon as may be."

Suitcases in hand, Ace, Gooper, and Tombstone strolled downhill toward the sparkling Mediterranean Sea. The city hummed with movement. Roman stonework blended with Renaissance arches and sculptures. Growing between the ancient edifices like hasty fungus, plain wood-framed buildings squatted.

The buildings grew taller as they neared the waterfront. A group of market women giggled and pointed at the party.

"They're laughin' atcha, Gooper," Tombstone crowed.

"Nawww. They're laughing at *yew*, stilts-for-legs."

"Rhinoceros."

"Stork."

The two exchanged fearsome scowls.

At the waterfront, a hundred ships crowded the docks. Ace stopped a sailor and asked for directions in Italian. Shortly, they found the *Neptune*, a stubby steamship with its hull painted blue.

As they trooped up the gangplank, Ace said, "Miles Fairweather is an Egyptologist and author of three books. The one about mummies is popular in English bookstores. He is a colleague of Sam's at the British Museum, though, like Sam, he is seldom actually resident in London."

"Wot's 'e look like?"

Ace shrugged. "No idea."

But in practice, it was obvious: Fairweather was the one who looked least like a sailor. A tallish white man in bush jacket and boots spotted the trio coming aboard and sauntered to meet them.

Fairweather's appearance was disarmingly ordinary. A paunch rolled over his belt. Brown hair curled atop a round face that would be at home on the local baker. He shook hands with all three warmly. "Greetings, greetings! I had a telegram about one of you, but I see three?"

Ace glanced at Tombstone and Gooper. "I do hope it's not an imposition."

"A surprise, but a pleasant one, I'm sure. Everyone who pulls their weight is welcome. Do make yourselves at home and so on, though I'm afraid this is a working trip, not a holiday cruise. Comforts may be few and far between."

Ace said, "Thank you for the welcome. I'm glad Mr. Entwhistle's assurances were accurate."

Tombstone said, "Don't worry none about comforts. Only Gooper here's gonna whine."

"Wot? Bah!" Gooper's red mustache and eyebrows bristled at Tombstone in incredulity.

Fairweather scanned Gooper's bulging shoulders and biceps. "To me, he looks most, erm, capable."

Ace said, "We are very glad you will admit some amateur archaeologists into the expedition, Doctor

Fairweather. We'll do our best to be of help, not of harm. Perhaps Mr. Entwhistle mentioned it to you already, but we also wish to find Sam Biming."

Fairweather's bland forehead wrinkled. "Sam Biming? Find?"

"He disappeared a few days ago."

"Sam Biming disappeared? You don't say! It's hard to get news when the local papers are in Italian." Fairweather wagged his head from side to side.

Ace said, "The only clues are some solid gold ankhs that came from the site you are investigating. The site we are going to."

"The dig site? You don't say! I'm speechless." Fairweather blew air into his cheeks and gestured impotently.

"None of it rings a bell, then?" Gooper's mustache drooped.

"No! How can the new dig site have anything to do with someone gone missing in London? I'm at a loss."

Ace's face lengthened in a worried frown that rivaled Tombstone for sheer forboding pessimism. "We're hanging out on a limb, too. Perhaps you should confer with Mr. Entwhistle. He persuaded us that there was something to this long-distance chase."

"That, I will. That, I will, indeed!" promised Fairweather. His eyes crinkled in suspicion.

The *Neptune* was a wide vessel with a shallow draft for easy passage on the Nile. Some of the other towering piles of cargo dwarfed the more modest mass of crates packed by the archaeologists. As the ship cleared the harbor and accelerated full steam toward Cairo, Ace inspected the crates. The largest stood eight feet high. Vertical slats with gaps between formed the outer shell. Another layer of interior slats filled the cracks. The well-ventilated construction was odd enough to catch Ace's eye.

The pilot scanned her surroundings. Sure enough, Darby Entwhistle was in sight, pretending not to be watching Ace. She marched toward his bulkhead lurking-place.

He straightened up and tugged on his lapels. A sunny grin broke out on his tanned face. "Miss Carroway, you are looking wonderful. Perhaps the sea air agrees with you. Fair weather for a fair journey, eh?"

"Mm." Ace gestured toward the largest crate. "What's in that big one?"

"That? I'm not completely sure, but it's probably the truck."

"You're bringing a truck?"

"It's a serious expedition, Miss Carroway." Entwhistle held his head high, and his regular features settled into a self-satisfied half-smile.

"All I see is you and Dr. Fairweather so far. Do you plan on adding to your crew?"

"Besides yourself and your, erm, colorful companions, you mean?" The crow's feet at the corners of Darby's eyes crinkled. "Well, have you met Bareem? No, probably not. He's very quiet."

"Bareem? That sounds anything but British."

"Ha-ha! Indeed, he is from, well, not too far from Thebes as a matter of fact."

"I'll keep an eye out for him. Anyone else?"

"Yes, the expedition will grow, but that comes later. We still have distance to cover."

Ace locked eyes with Entwhistle. "Tell me about the dig."

Entwhistle raised a finger and waggled it. "I *am* sorry, Miss Carroway, but it must be kept secret. Let it be a surprise for you when we get there. Trust me. It's astounding. It's sensational, and I'm understating the impact."

Ace tried a smile. "Surely, you can tell *me*."

Darby swallowed, his eyes widening. "Oh, Miss Carroway, how I want to. *How* I want to."

The hours dragged on so slowly that even the Mediterranean seascape lost its charm. For Ace, Gooper, and Tombstone, fretting about Sam only frayed already-prickly nerves. Conversations sputtered to silence.

The discovery of the lurker was, therefore, a welcome relief. Gooper spotted an idle man in the shadow of an air intake watching Ace. The next hour, Ace saw a dark figure lean to observe Tombstone. Later, Tombstone eyed a dark-skinned fellow curling his lip, aiming the sneer at Gooper from behind. Perhaps Darby Entwhistle had eyes for Ace alone, but the lurker seemed equally curious about all three of the Carroway party.

The three conferred up in the bow. Gooper said,

"'E's dressed like a sailor. Trousers an' shirt. But 'e's not working."

Ace said, "Bare feet. Wiry frame. About forty years of age."

Tombstone readjusted his Stetson. "He's got a glare on 'im that could curdle milk. Gooper. Hate to break this to ya, but that feller don't like you. Not one bit."

Ace laughed. "Fellas. Honestly."

Gooper thumbed his nose at Tombstone, then slapped a fist into an open palm. "So. Three of us. One of 'im. Shall we interview the gent?"

A smile still lingered on Ace's face. "Yes, shall we?"

They found the idle man midship, watching Dr. Fairweather from the shadowy side of the bridge. He didn't *hide*, exactly, but he employed a degree of furtive stealth. At the approach of the three allies, his eyes darted left and right. Seeing no escape, his jaw tightened and he glared at them as if their very existence angered him.

"Greetin's, mate." Gooper's mustache stayed flatly horizontal.

Ace said, "Ace Carroway. This is Gooper. Tombstone. Are you Bareem?"

The umber skin on his shaved head gleamed, but his scowl only deepened. His face worked as if he might spit upon the trio, but he spat only words. "Yes, yes. Bareem. Do not talk to Bareem. We have no talk." His English halted and stuttered, colored by an accent not even Ace recognized.

"You are with Dr. Fairweather's expedition. We're just introducing ourselves." Ace planted fists on her wide belt.

Bareem's frown deepened.

"Howdy, pardner." Tombstone grinned. The gleam of teeth enhanced his skeletal aspect.

Bareem made push gestures with his empty hands. "Go. Go from me."

Ace studied him for a moment, then shrugged. "All right. See you around, Bareem."

The wiry man lowered his voice. "Go from ship at Cairo. Do not come back."

"What?" Ace's eyebrows shot up.

Bareem favored them with an especially sour glare, then turned his back on them. Bare feet slapped the deck as he stalked away.

The flummoxed allies watched him go.

Gooper summed up. "It's not just me, lizard man. The bloke don't like *any* of us."

Chapter 12

In the wee hours of the night, the ship stopped in Tripoli for more cargo, but the captain kept the boilers warm. By the time the sun rose, the *Neptune* had already churned through a hundred miles of open water toward the mouth of the Nile.

Midway through this second day, Tombstone and Gooper exhausted all the charms of playing with cards. Tombstone yawned big and regarded his chesty friend with eyes half lidded. "I'm gonna regret askin' this, I bet, but what was that beast you wanted to see in Egypt? Tore-a-heart beast or somethin'."

Gooper's red mustache bristled upward into a dreamy smile. "It's the tora hartebeest. Rarest of the rare. I don't know a soul 'oo's seen 'er."

Tombstone scratched under the brim of his Stetson. "So, what is it? Sounds scary."

"Naw! Not scary. It's a big antelope. Africa's got a lot of different antelope, but the tora hartebeest's as big as a kudu. Big, an' beautiful."

"Why're you so excited about a ol' antelope?"

Gooper blinked, injured. "Tombstone. The tora hartebeest is not *just* an antelope. It's an unstudied branch of zoology. Why, it could be a missin' link, or a new branch of mammalia. We know nothin' of it, not 'ow it mates, not 'ow it breeds, not 'ow it finds food, not 'ow far it ranges. Nothin'!"

Tombstone let the deck of cards fall into his shirt

pocket and stood up. "All right, pardner. I can see how this here tora hartebeest's important to ya. When we get there, I'll help ya spot one."

Gooper's mustache curved upwards again. "That's right straight of yew, mate."

The tall man's dour face almost smiled back; at least he looked less mournful than average for a moment. He yawned again and ambled out on deck.

The Westerner decided to guarantee a quiet nap by climbing into one of the lifeboats. He stretched his lanky frame to full length along the centerline, basking in the Mediterranean sun and quite invisible to all but the seagulls. He pulled his Stetson down over his eyes. His eyes drifted closed.

The steam engines throbbed. Seagulls called, their strident shrieks attenuated to melody by distance and the fickle breezes. The sunlight cooked the skyward halves of his denim trousers. He dozed.

Voices leaked into his consciousness, both male.

"What *possessed* you, Darby? Think of the risk!"

"Soon, we'll be beyond risk as you well know. Besides, I didn't start it. The *kekewe-saew* did by taking Biming captive. It'll all work out when we reach Kush."

Tombstone fought the warmth and soothing sounds and struggled awake. Sleepy eyes threw off their heavy lids and stared into his own hat. English inflections colored both voices.

"Yes, yes, fine. Getting to Kush will solve a lot. But, still, you're an idiot. Even now I don't think you have a clue what a tiger you've got by the tail. *We've* got by the tail. I can't believe you didn't recognize the name Cecilia Carroway. Anybody that studies *Who's*

Who as closely as you do should know Ace Carroway!"

"Stop harping on it, Bertram! I'm caught up with the news, now, all right? I knew she was amazing, though, the first time I saw her. What a woman."

"Stop slobbering, you dolt. In your dizzy state of mind you can't see the obvious. Think. She's not exactly falling for you head over heels, is she? She's too rich to be bribed. And she's dangerous."

"Bertram, Bertram. You worry too much. I've got her hooked. I've got her by the curiosity bump."

"Well, what about those two brutes? That musclebound one isn't as stupid as he looks."

In the lifeboat, Tombstone raised his hat to stare at the cerulean sky. His lips formed silent words. "Yes he is."

Darby said, "So far, it's working out fine. Like I say, we'll be untouchable soon enough."

The voices decreased in volume as if they were walking away.

"Yes, yes. Well, I'll be nervous until we get to Kush, that's for sure. If something happens it'll be your fault, Darby. Are you sure the boat from Cairo will be ready for us?"

Tombstone fretted over the voice named Darby. Despite the name and broadly British accent, it didn't trigger Tombstone's recollection of Darby Entwhistle's way of speaking. The diction seemed a mixture of Entwhistle and Gooper. In slow motion to keep the lifeboat from rocking, Tombstone levered his body up and peeked over the edge of the lifeboat gunwale.

No one. They were gone.

The cowpoke-electrician's weather-beaten face wrinkled in perplexity. "Who th' heck is Bertram?"

♠ ♠ ♠

"I think I heard 'em say that the *kekewe-saew* kidnapped Sam." Tombstone, Gooper, and Ace huddled between stacks of crates to confer in private.

Gooper's red bushes of eyebrows squirmed. "The jesters to the bloody pharaoh? Three thousand years dead?"

Tombstone slid his eyes over to Gooper. "It's what I heard."

Ace watched a high seagull sail in the gap between crate stacks. "And a second mention of Kush, whatever or wherever it lies. I think we should open our minds to some odd possibilities. Perhaps there is a group that has revived ancient Egyptian rituals. Or invented new rituals." She lowered her head to placidly examine her associates. She splayed her fingers out wide. "Such as twenty-four trails of blood."

Tombstone shifted his weight and cleared his throat. "Are we chasin' down the right trail?"

Ace answered immediately. "Yes. Murky as the path may be, I think we chose wisely. At Cairo, I had decided to give Entwhistle an ultimatum to tell us concrete information or we would quit the expedition. But what Tombstone overheard makes me think there is substance to his hints."

"I ain't positive it was Entwhistle's voice."

"Regardless," Ace said. "Even if the voices were men we have not yet seen, it starts to stink of conspiracy."

"Oo!" Gooper's mustache curved happily up. "More 'eads to crack?"

"Bloodthirsty Brit," Tombstone said.

Ace looked upward once more. "I see a flock of terns. We approach the Nile delta."

Chapter 13

The *Nautilus* hooked right at the Nile delta and churned up the shipping lane dredged through swamps and farmlands. The sun set over Cairo in orange glory as they tied up at a riverside dock. The throb of engines died away, and a fainter city ambiance tickled the eardrums. Atop the silhouettes of minarets, the keening calls of muezzin called the faithful to prayer. Distant, invisible camels did their best to disrupt the ritual, adding their brays to the palette of city noises.

Darby Entwhistle and Miles Fairweather stayed to oversee the transfer of cargo to a shallow-bottomed river cruise ship. The Carroway party was obliged to find lodging for the night in Cairo itself, so the three filtered in among buildings still warm from the day's heat. Tombstone's jaw went slack and stayed slack as they navigated alien streets, and his eyes stared. He leapt back to avoid a collision with a camel and almost lost his Stetson. "Good gravy!" He reset his hat and stared after the camel and its driver. "That is the ugliest horse I ever set eyes on!"

Gooper scrunched his face at Tombstone. "It's a camel. *Camelus dromedarius.*"

"I know that, ya squat toad. And it's the ugliest horse I ever set eyes on."

They dodged tent awnings and more camels and a great diversity of passers-by dressed in everything from Scottish kilts to leopard skins to turbans and robes.

Tombstone muttered, "Well, I'll be!" and "Whillikers!" and "I ain't never seen the like."

Ace sniffed out a telegraph office, but it was closed. Perhaps it closed every evening.

In contrast, all of the hotels eagerly sought lodgers, and the party was enthusiastically ushered into one called Al-Tair. As soon as she was alone, Ace opened her transmitter suitcase on the bed. Tapping a key, Ace dit-dahed a Morse code message on *Sky Arrow One's* frequency. The airship answered immediately. Joyce Harcourt reported an all-safe and that the *Sky Arrow* was operating perfectly. Ace asked that the aeronauts stop at a Cairo telegraph office to send inquiries. The Scotland Yard report on the blood spatter from the alley keenly interested Ace. She also requested a physical description of Miles Fairweather.

Sky Arrow One had already baked through a desert day at the airport when the Morse code message came through. In the gloriously cool pool of shade beneath the gas bag, the silver gondola gleamed gold, reflecting the ambient soil. It cooled even more through the night, but as the naked sun rose, Harcourt, Vivian, and Gilbert emerged to start their chores.

By mid-morning, *Sky Arrow One* was fueled and watered, but Harcourt needed to send telegrams. Furthermore, she worried about the sufficiency of their provisions. The three began walking to the bazaar.

The length of the dusty road daunted them. A savvy cab driver noticed their facial expressions as he passed, and he halted to speak with them. They soon succumbed to the sales technique of "Akbar" and the temptation of his horse-drawn cab. The purple-turbaned dynamo spoke enough English to flirt outrageously with Joyce Harcourt.

"Your eyes are like desert sapphires," Akbar extolled. He paid no attention to driving. His horse seemed to know the way.

"If I had a son, he'd be your age," Harcourt protested.

"Your hair is like golden flax of Nefertiti," sang Akbar.

"We're going to the telegraph office." Harcourt's face colored with more than a simple blush of sun exposure.

"Your arms are like the reeds of the Nile that bend in the ebb and flow!"

"Oh, I give up."

Vivian and Gilbert exchanged grins.

Akbar's dust-caked horse wove through increasing traffic of animals, people, and a few cars. It came to a stop and snorted. The small mud-walled structure blended in with dozens nearby, but a small shingle identified it as a branch of the Eastern Telegraph Company.

Akbar's grin faded. "Stupid animal, you should have gone the long way. Now, the goodbye is too soon." With a flourish of robe sleeves, the purple dervish offered a helping hand to Harcourt as she stepped down from the open buggy.

"Thank you, Akbar," Harcourt said.

"Queen of my heart, I am ever your servant. For

five piastres more, I would be your servant even be-yond death." Akbar sank to one knee imploringly.

Harcourt's smile grew strained. "I don't need a servant that long." She blinked. "But, wait. Akbar, I'll give you another piastre if you help Vivian and Gilbert shop for some dry food for our trip."

Akbar heaved a theatrical sigh and spread his robed hands in resignation. "Memsahib, I hear and obey. I will escort them to the bazaar, and no filthy merchant shall cheat them."

Harcourt placed a coin in his ready palm and fled into the telegraph office.

Akbar touched his purple turban and bowed to the white-clad duo. "May fortune smile upon you, young masters."

Vivian stifled a giggle. Gilbert chuckled unabashed-ly. "Akbar, you're the best. Can you help us buy food? Commodore Harcourt will be some time."

"It is good you notice! Yes, I am the best." Akbar salaamed again. "As for food, we will make Al-Hassan's cart heavy with it."

"Great!" said Gilbert.

"Ha! Ha! Are you a Yankee, young master?"

Gilbert glanced at Vivian. Vivian shrugged. Gilbert said, "I guess so. We're from Pennsylvania."

"Is that in America?"

Gilbert blinked. "Yes."

"Then you are a Yankee."

Vivian said, "Good to know. Where's the food?"

"The bazaar is by the river, young miss. Al-Hassan will take us there. In, in, in."

The twins climbed back into the roofless cab. Gil-bert murmured to his sister, "Should we go to the river? The Fairweather expedition is there, somewhere."

Vivian rolled a nonchalant shoulder. "I don't think it matters if we are seen. In any case, they should be gone already."

Al-Hassan rolled them a few blocks farther, into thickening crowds of colorful people. Akbar's gaudy robe and turban paled in comparison to some of the vivid colors swirling around them. Akbar tied Al-Hassan by a drinking trough and in the next hour taught the twins how to barter at market. They bought cheese, butter, wheat flour, dried dates, crackers, nuts, and oil.

When all was stowed in the buggy, Vivian fanned herself. "Hot, now! I see the crowd has thinned."

Akbar beamed. "Young mistress, you have eyes like an eagle. No sane man suns himself at noon. Is it time for coffee?"

Gilbert said, "I guess so. We didn't buy any drinks, yet."

"Come, come, come, come! Akbar knows the best coffee."

Vivian hissed, "Gilbert, you don't know a thing about coffee."

The lad spread his hands. "So? We're about to learn."

Within sight of Al-Hassan, who appeared to be dozing, they ducked under a tent awning into blissful shade. Café tables and chairs beckoned, and Akbar slid a chair for Vivian. A shy smile touched her stoic face.

Akbar rattled off an order in rapid Egyptian Arabic. He leaned back in his chair and wiggled his eyebrows up and down. "I order it half-sweet. I think you will like it."

Three tiny cups and a small ornate pitcher of coffee arrived. The server, a short, round matron in a scarf and practical desert-dweller robes, poured the steaming brown liquid out for them all.

Akbar salaamed to her. "Thank you, Zebe!" He raised his shapely little cup. "Toast, yes? A toast to success and long life."

They clinked their tiny cups, and each sipped.

Akbar's lips curved upward in bliss.

Gilbert's nose crinkled, and his eyes squinted.

Vivian's eyes widened, and she sat bolt upright.

Both Akbar and Gilbert eyed her with concern. Vivian maintained her stiff posture for several moments. Akbar ventured, "Young miss? Is everything well?"

"Well," she whispered.

Gilbert and Akbar exchanged glances.

She shook off her stupor and flashed a toothy grin. "Very well. It's powerful. It's potent. It's rich. It makes Mother's seem like weak, bitter tea."

"I'm glad one of us likes it." Gilbert rubbed a finger on his temple.

Akbar studied them and sipped his own coffee. Gilbert ignored the remainder of his drink and scanned the colorful crowd. Vivian took a second sip of hers with an air of religious reverence. Akbar steepled his fingers philosophically. "Only a fool expects success in all things."

The server Zebe watched all this with hands on her generous hips. She spoke rapidly in the local dialect. Akbar held up a hand to stop her. "Zebe. You know English. These are Americans. What was that about blood?"

Zebe huffed. "Akbar. I only wondered if you had been to see it. If you don't hurry, they might wash it away."

"See what? Where?"

Zebe shook a finger at him. "Akbar, it is said that you have twenty eyes and twenty ears, but this day you need twenty-one."

"Woman. Do not sour my coffee. Tell me."

"At the obelisk of Amenhotep by the river. Blood like a starburst all over the stones. And people last night heard terrible screams, but no one seems missing."

84

Chapter 14

About the time Vivian first tasted sweetened Egyptian coffee, Ace Carroway stood upon the deck of a steamer cruising up the Nile. Shaded by a wide-brimmed hat, the gold hues of her eyes darkened to a steely luster as she gazed into the distance.

There they stood, the great pyramids of Giza. From atop their plateau, the ancient sentinels overlooked the city and the wide Nile. Distance erased the erosions of time and the morning sun lit evident perfection of architecture.

Ace's thoughts spun through webs of years. She reviewed once again the new-yet-ancient array of golden ankhs in her mind's eye. Crimson stars of twenty-four points floated over the face of Sam Biming. "A ritual of time, death, and rebirth," she muttered, "but I can't see how it necessarily involves theft or kidnapping."

She stood by herself next to the largest of crates, the one that held a truck. Her bronzed hand lightly grasped a slat of the crate for security. The crate took up so much space, only a mere yard of deck remained to stand upon. The deck had no safety rail; any stumble could easily result in a tumble into the river.

An extrasensory prickle ran up her back, and her eyes darted forward. Darby Entwhistle leaned on the lounge-house, packing his pipe. His eyes lay on his tobacco, but his sandy hair bounced in such a way that Ace was sure he had, a moment ago, been looking at her.

Ace's nose wrinkled.

The wind shifted for a moment, eddying from the east instead of the west. It brought a tang of unwashed bodies, but the fleeting scent disappeared in a moment. Ace's nose unwrinkled, and she stared at her hand as it rested on the large crate.

The expedition crates filled most of the back half of the little shallow-bottomed steamer. The unmarked boat seemed to have no name, and its three sullen Egyptian crewmen gave no names, either.

Ahead of the cargo pile sat the boiler, then a lounge topped with a wheelhouse. No glass filled the airy windowpanes of the lounge, and its shaded and drafty interior provided a refuge from the relentless sun. Forward of the lounge, a pair of cabins flanked a lavatory. The limited amenities would become intimately familiar: a thousand miles remained to be traversed on the sinuous back of the mighty Nile.

Tombstone gazed until the pyramids disappeared astern. Wishing for a respite from Gooper, he quit the lounge and ambled to the back of the boat, but Bareem coiled there like a silent rattlesnake. He went forward, but one of the crewmen already occupied the bow. The wheelhouse disqualified itself, and the cabins were dark and stuffy. Besides side decks only a yard wide, the crowded lounge was evidently the only place to rest.

Tombstone scratched his unshaven chin. "Dingnab it. This ship is tighter than a girth cinch[1]."

---

[1] On a western saddle, the front strap that secures the saddle to the horse. The rear one is the flank cinch.

Ace solved her own privacy problem with quiet efficiency and nested atop the pile of crates. The crew noticed her halfway through her daily exercises. They stared with slack jaws from the wheelhouse. The ship began drifting off course.

Darby Entwhistle stormed from the lounge. He whipped around to face forward and snapped, "Eyes forward! You shall behave as gentleman while under my employ!"

After a sullen second, one replied, "Aye, aye." Sluggishly, they turned to face the bow, and soon the ship steered a proper course. Ace herself seemed not to notice and continued her torturous calisthenics.

Darby pleaded, "Miss Carroway, would you please consider, erm, not being so high?"

"I am fine, here." Ace balanced on one hand, for a moment resembling a mutant mushroom with a stem of one arm.

"Please come down? I am concerned."

"Your concern is noted, Mr. Entwhistle."

Gooper emerged from the lounge to eye Entwhistle from beneath bristly red eyebrows. He shortly invented his own solution to the privacy issue. He employed his apelike arms to clamber atop the lounge, behind the wheelhouse. The flat rectangle of tin supported his weight, and he squatted there, cheery in his bowler hat.

Tombstone exited the lounge and dodged a dangling hobnailed boot. He squinted back and upward at Gooper. "Yer gettin' double sun there, pardner. You'll get sunburn so bad that you'll go lobster red."

"Desist, cow person of Yankeedom," Gooper effected a noble air. "I am spotting *Crocodylus niloticus*."

"Uh. Whut?"

"The Nile crocodile," said Ace from her stack of crates. "Tombstone, remember I handed you Sam's book about the Coptic language? Could you dig that up for me?"

"Shore, Ace. Gimme a minute."

And so the nameless steamer chugged upstream. Ace read her linguistics treatise. Gooper scanned for wildlife. Tombstone paced, his boots clacking in wooden rhythm around the deck.

The boat kept near the channel center. The river shores were ragged lines of green and brown a quarter-mile away either left or right. A slow parade of farmlands and towns glided by, much the same hour to hour.

When evening fell, Ace waved off invitations to sleep in the cabins. She curled up instead on top of the cargo crates. Fairweather and Entwhistle frowned and muttered to each other over the matter. To their evident consternation, even promises of an entire cabin to herself could not entice her to find a different bed.

Fading twilight uncovered diamond-hard stars. The ship chugged on in the darkness. Tombstone tapped a light bulb in the gloom-filled lounge and asked the shadowy figure of a crewman. "Hey, feller. What's wrong with the lights?"

The shadow changed shape in what was probably a shrug. "No electricity."

Tombstone's mouth flattened. "Yeah? Well. We'll see."

The ship chugged on through the starry night, throbbing forward through the lazy flow of the Nile. No electric light burned, but a red glow could be seen in the doorway of the lounge from time to time. When the red glow pulsed, it faintly illuminated eddies of pipe smoke and the profile of Darby Entwhistle. He leaned in the door frame, yearning eyes on an indistinct catlike form reposing atop the cargo.

Chapter 15

Next morning, Gooper holed up in the shaded lounge, a changed man. His pale hands and face had bloomed scarlet, a shade even brighter than his red hair. With his eyes shut, he lay unmoving, except for the occasional, soulful moan.

Luckily for Gooper, Tombstone had begun tracing the wiring of the ship and thus had no time for teasing. As regards to sunburn, Tombstone remained serenely untroubled under his wide-brimmed Stetson.

Ace descended from her crates and skirted the boiler to enter the lounge. After a double-take at Gooper, she reversed her path. She soon returned with a lump of cocoa butter and directed the biologist to smear it on the affected areas.

Miles Fairweather sunnily commented, "Surely, we've got an extra pith helmet for you, old chap. A bowler hat's not much help in the sun."

Tombstone ducked his head in the doorway. "Ding-nab it. Doctor Fairweather, these here boat fellers don't speak a lot of English. I want a toolbox. The generator's stuck. Should be an easy job, greasin' her shafts. Then we'd have 'lectricity again."

"I'll see what I can do," Fairweather answered.

They left together, but not before Tombstone shot a grin at Gooper. "Nice lobster disguise. Very convincing."

"Bugger off," Gooper growled.

Tombstone set up shop. He disassembled and cleaned the steam-turbine generator attached to the boiler. Because it was the only action aboard ship, a small crowd gathered around him.

Darby Entwhistle used the opportunity to sidle up beside Ace. She managed a weak smile. "Good morning, Mr. Entwhistle."

"Good morning, Miss Carroway. Lovely day."

As Entwhistle chatted up Ace, the hot, sunny day commenced. Much like the day before, and the day before that.

After an hour, Tombstone enjoyed a moment of adulation when the revitalized generator whirred to life. After the round of applause, the crowd broke up. Lunch came and went, and most succumbed to a round of naps. Ace, in particular, curled up in the shady lounge and immediately plunged into a deep slumber.

Unfortunately for the rapid progress of the steamer, the urge for naps extended to the wheelhouse. The pilot slumped over the wheel, and the boat's rudder stayed fixed. The course of the mighty Nile, however, did not run so straight. A quarter of an hour later, a slithery scrape at the bow accompanied a deceleration such that everyone rolled forward. To cap it off, a violent shudder from the screw thrummed through the ship. The engine moaned like a heretic on the torture rack and screeched to an unwilling halt.

The pilot blearily raised his head. People boiled out of the lounge, rubbing their eyes and stumbling in bewilderment.

"Egaf maharrakat![2]" called a clear, decisive voice.

In the wheelhouse, the pilot flipped a lever. The engine stopped straining. In the quiet, the facts became obvious. The ship had run aground on the western shore in a swampy area. No cultivated lands or houses lay near though it was hard to see far. The wild area was thick with cattails and rushes at least twice as tall as a man.

The commanding voice had been Ace's, and now she padded aft to peer over the stern into the waters at the back of the boat.

Darby Entwhistle leveled a finger at the pilot who stood in the wheelhouse rubbing his forehead. "Look what you've done, you fool!"

Ace called from the stern, "The screw tangled in a fishing net from what I can see." Shredded remnants of a net tumbled in slow motion beneath the surface of the water. A few liberated glass floats bobbed on the surface, now bound for Cairo and the Mediterranean Sea.

"Well?" queried Miles Fairweather, his round, good-natured face bemused.

"Yes. Well?" Entwhistle echoed, eyeing each of the three crew. The trio wore carefully expressionless faces and stayed mute.

Ace cheerfully called, "Tombstone? Lend me your knife and get your pistol. You get to keep the crocodiles off me." She began shucking off her boots.

"Oo! Action!" Gooper adjusted his borrowed pith helmet, which resembled half a beehive with a wide brim attached, and cracked his knuckles. "Need any

---

[2] "Stop the engines!"

'elp down there, Ace?"

Tombstone handed Ace his Bowie knife, its blade about five inches long. Ace answered Gooper, "I'll let you know in a minute." She clamped the knife between her teeth and dived over the stern of the steamer. A moment later, only ripples remained of her splash-less entry point into the Nile.

"What? What?" Entwhistle's eyes flew wide, and his mouth gaped, aghast.

Gooper nudged the Englishman's shoulder playfully, nearly knocking him over the side in the process. "Get used to it, guv. She's the ace."

In a minute, Tombstone had retrieved his Smith & Wesson six-shooter from his luggage. He held it loosely in his right hand as his eyes speared here and there in the water, scanning for crocodiles or other threats. Ace hadn't come up, yet.

Darby Entwhistle clutched at Gooper's thick forearm. "Where is she? Is she trapped? Is she drowned?"

Gooper pulled his arm free. "Guv. It's *Ace*, like I says."

Ace erupted from the river at that moment and gulped several lungsful of air.

"Oh, gracious!" Entwhistle breathed.

Ace waved her borrowed knife and sang out, "It's a snarl. But I'd say two or three more dives, and the propeller will be free to turn again. Somebody drop me a rope, please, so I can climb back aboard."

With that, she jackknifed her body into a dive, her shoeless feet disappearing last.

The crew, shoddy as they may be, managed to scrounge a rope. One of them put a few knots in it, and looped it over a cleat. Ace came up for air and dove again.

Tombstone caught movement toward the middle of the Nile, and he swiveled to face it. After a moment, he said, "It's a croc. But it's swimmin' away. Afraid o' my six-gun, mebbe."

Gooper snorted. "Afraid of your breath, p'raps, mate."

Tombstone frowned at Gooper, then his eyes darted every direction. "What's that splashin' sound?"

His words elevated the men's perceptions. Suddenly, they all realized that a watery rushing sound had been getting louder for some time. As they wondered and stared, the splashing grew and grew in volume. It surrounded them, and their ears could perceive no clear direction of origin.

Ace broke the surface just as the frothing watery sounds amplified to storm levels, though no cloud graced the dome of the sky. Off the bow of the steamer, the reeds and rushes tossed as if a gale tore through them. The disturbance approached the ship. The splashing became a roar.

"Hippopotamus," Ace panted. She spotted the dangling knotted rope and turned toward it.

Cattails parted for huge brown shapes charging forward. Water splashed high as giant cloven hoofs plunged like pistons. Blunt snouts preceded massive bodies. There seemed a hundred of them, though a cooler head might put the count at forty of the primeval beasts.

At sight of the boat, several hippopotamuses bawled like skewered bagpipes. A chorus of grunts broke out from the remainder of the charging ungulates. The herd parted around the small ship, engulfing it.

Ace swam a few strokes toward the rope dangling from the steamer, but it was clear she would not reach it before the front line of the herd.

A massive adult charged Ace, opening a four-foot-wide jaw. Ace's eyes popped wide, and she ducked under the water. The hippopotamus promptly dived too. Both Ace and her animal pursuer disappeared from view for those on deck.

"Ace!" Gooper cried.

His voice was all but lost in the thunder of the herd. They swarmed past the boat, buffeting it. Tombstone lost his footing and fell hard on the deck.

In seconds, the herd galloped past and descended into the waters of the Nile. Soon, only their backs, skulls, and wiggly ears could be seen.

Ace did not appear.

Gooper shouted at the water, "Hey! You! Get away!"

A submerged brown blob hovered near. At Gooper's shout, far from fleeing, it nosed toward the ship. The bump of impact sent several men tumbling.

Tombstone recovered his footing and made his way to the side. "Ain't no overgrown water pig gonna eat Ace Carroway!"

With that pronouncement, he pointed his pistol downward and fired a steady stream of six bullets. Perhaps it was the sharp sound of the shots alone, or perhaps some of the slugs connected and caused the beast pain. In any case, the animal moved off toward the Nile, staying beneath the surface.

And nothing else moved.

"Where is Miss Carroway?" Entwhistle said. His

eyes probed the muddied waters.

"Ace?" Gooper called. His ham fists clenched.

Tombstone's dour face took on a pale hue under his leathery tan.

The crew and the archaeologists milled around as the long seconds stretched longer.

"Ace…" Gooper pleaded.

98

CHAPTER 16

The rope ladder twitched.

"You called?" Arm over arm and panting, the waterlogged flyer clambered up to the deck. Gooper and Tombstone caught her by the upper arms and hauled her up until she stood on her feet.

"Oh. Whew!" Darby Entwhistle said.

"See? No water pig's gonna get Ace," said Tombstone.

"That *Hippopotamus amphibius* wanted a bite of yew, ma'am," Gooper said. "'Ow did yew thwart its dastardly ambition, eh?"

"I wriggled down under the boat is all. Into the narrow space between the hull and river bottom."

A wrinkle appeared between Gooper's fluffy eyebrows. "An' you 'eld your breath."

Ace shook droplets from her unkempt hair and grinned. "Swimming's alright, but I do prefer flying."

Ace declared the screw liberated from the fishing net. The engine was engaged in reverse. After a moment of doubt, the steamer slid free. They resumed their journey south against the current.

♠ ♠ ♠

On the second evening, Ace hunkered down at the apex of the pile of crates and extended the antenna of her suitcase-radio. Tombstone and Gooper joined her, standing arm in arm, acting as visual screens. Once again, *Sky Arrow One* replied instantly. Ace tapped and listened, tapped and listened. Finally, she disconnected the battery and lowered the antenna. She swiveled to peer at the starlit faces of Tombstone and Gooper.

"London reports that Sam has not been found. Also, the blood is animal, not human."

Gooper crossed his arms. "Blimey. Who died, then? I mean, who screamed? I swear by me dear old mum that scream was 'uman and not animal."

"I agree, pardner."

"I have no answer for that. But there's something else."

"Wot?"

"A physical description. Miles Fairweather is six foot, slender, 55, sandy hair, blue eyes."

They exchanged glances, eyebrows high.

"'Oo's the chubby dark-haired bloke wot *says* 'e's Miles Fairweather, then?" Gooper's bushy eyebrows danced.

"Maybe his real name is Bertram, the name I overheard before Cairo," Tombstone said.

"That is the simplest explanation," Ace said.

"The plot thickens," Tombstone said, not unhappily.

"One more thing," Ace said.

"Whut's that?"

"Another 24-pointed star of blood was placed near an obelisk in Cairo. It was the night we were there."

Tombstone rubbed his stubbly chin. "These blood star things relate to us, somehow?"

Gooper cracked his knuckles, one at a time. "Either we are followin' the blood sacrifice cult, or they are followin' us."

"Or we are traveling together," Ace said.

"Eh? What's that supposed to mean?"

"I can't be sure. I'll tell you as soon as I work it out. In the meantime, it's time to turn in. Goodnight, fellas."

Gooper and Tombstone each heaved sighs. They clambered down. They passed a pipe-puffing Darby Entwhistle. Their narrow-eyed death-stares probably went unobserved in the darkness.

Ace composed herself as if for sleep. She chose the same spot she chose the previous night: the corner of the very large crate. Like the previous night, she did not sleep. Instead, she slipped her screwdriver from her wide belt. She tapped three times on top of the crate. Her ear lay touching the wood of the crate's roof. Taps returned.

Ace smiled in the darkness. "Hello, Sam."

An hour later, Darby Entwhistle gave up his Ace-watching and retired. Only the night pilot appeared to be awake, judging by the fact that the steamer did not run aground again.

An hour after that, Ace got a surprise.

She prided herself on her sharp senses. After all, with her daily exercise regimen she honed them to ever-sharper acuity. But such was her concentration on her tap-tap-tapping that she was caught unaware.

The weight of the man pressed her against the crate as the cool edge of metal pressed across the flesh of her neck.

"Still!" hissed the urgent whisper. "I wish talk."

"Bareem," Ace said. She slipped into a Wing Chun mantra to control her breathing and her racing heart.

"Yes. I wish say this. Get off at Aswan."

The whites of his staring eyes swam in her peripheral vision. His breath whistled. As Ace's heart stopped its panicked leaps, she realized a truth: Bareem felt fear.

"I listen," Ace said.

"You did not go at Cairo. You *must* go at Aswan."

Ace took a second to answer. "Why?"

"I do you a favor!" Bareem's forehead and skull gleamed with sweat. "You have some skill and honor for a foreigner. I save your life by saying *go*."

"You save my life?"

"Go at Aswan, woman. Do not go to Kush. There is no escape from Kush. It is death. You understand? Death and worse than death."

"And if I stay?"

"Then you are stupid. And also, I will kill you. It will be kinder."

"Ah. Well, I guess I'll think it over."

The weight of him left her, and the touch of the blade vanished. She whipped her head around to see him retreat. As he backed away, he held his knife between him and the prone pilot.

Starlight gleamed on the knife in a peculiar way, soft yet sparkling. Ace blinked. The sheen was that of pure gold.

A moment later, Bareem jumped down from the crate.

Ace felt her own pulse. "What a shock! Well, I wasn't sleepy anyway, right?"

CHAPTER 17

Ace slept late, rousing as the steamer passed the majestic Luxor temple ruin, the heart of the city called Thebes in antiquity. The monumental columns and towering walls impressed even from mid-river. Modern Luxor had no buildings that competed in terms of grandeur.

As they were approaching Aswan, Bareem left his customary perch in the stern, presumably to nap. Ace motioned to Tombstone and Gooper. They followed her to the stern and huddled behind the crates out of sight.

Ace whispered, "Bareem and I had an interview last night. He is *disappointed* that we have not already cut ties with the Fairweather expedition. He wishes us to depart at Aswan."

Gooper blew air through his mustache. "Not that I like the stubby baldy, but I wouldn't mind. The crew're probably criminals. The bloke wot says 'e's Miles Fairweather is an imposter. And the way that Entwhistle bloke looks at you makes me want ter toss 'im overboard."

Ace's face drooped. She sighed.

Tombstone said, "Did the little feller say why?"

Ace said, "Not specifically. He implied that we were heading for a location called Kush, from which there is no escape. He underscored his point by holding a solid gold knife to my neck."

"Wot? I'll tie the blighter in a knot."

Ace held up a finger. "Shh. Not so loud. Also, yes, let's watch each other's backs. But although his methods were clumsy and brutish, I think his intentions are sincere. He wishes to save us from going to Kush, which he equates with a fate worse than death."

Tombstone narrowed his eyes. "Kush is where Darby Entwhistle said we're headin' to, and it's the old name for Nubia. So, it's a real place?"

"It is. Sam confirmed it," she said.

Gooper and Tombstone stared at Ace.

"Sam?" said Tombstone.

"Sam?" said Gooper.

Ace grinned. She held a finger to her lips. She continued, her voice barely audible over the steady growl of the engine. "I got curious about the biggest crate. The one with double rows of slats. It's a fine, sturdy design, excellent for ventilation. Darby said it contained a truck. My nose told me otherwise when I stood downwind. I smelled perfume, and, erm, humans. Humans a bit too long between baths."

"Wot?" Gooper's mouth dropped open.

"Shh! Keep it down!" Tombstone reprimanded, then echoed, "What, now?"

Ace smiled faintly. "Well, it could have been dirty laundry, but I suspected not. I've been sleeping, or pretending to sleep, on top of the crates as you have seen. What I've been doing a lot of, however, is tapping. Tapping Morse code. Sam's been tapping back."

"Well, shove a bit in my mouth an' call me busted!" Tombstone marveled.

"He's a bit miserable, but he's uninjured. He is forbidden from talking out loud. He has company and plenty of it. Four citizens of a place called Meroë-inet are also riding out the journey in the crate. They consider themselves the heirs of the kingdom of Meroë. I think Meroë is simply an older-still name for Kush or Nubia. The four are holding Sam prisoner."

"Are we gonna bust 'im outta there?" Tombstone asked.

"Sam begs us not to. He says we need to rescue Prince Saret. We can't do that unless we go to Kush."

Tombstone's long face lengthened. "Saw-Rett? Who's Prince Saret?"

Ace's face twitched in a feeble smile. "Bear with me. I may not have this right. Sam is having some trouble with the language, although the Nubians are quite willing to whisper. He says that communication is easier every day. Anyway, here goes. Apparently, Re-pat Saret, that is, Prince Saret, is by bloodline the next pharaoh. However, he is being held prisoner in Meroë-inet by someone named Thubis. Thubis has claimed the throne."

"So Thubis pulled a coup, an' now 'e's Pharaoh of Meroë-inet. Am I keeping up?" Gooper wondered.

"Yes. Good work. Now, the people in the crate are *kekewe-saew*, the jester-assassins of the pharaoh. Darby Entwhistle already described them to us. Little did we know how direct his experience was! Presumably, they are being kept out of sight so as not to attract attention. I'm not sure exactly how Bareem fits in. He might be a *kekewe-saew* himself, or he might be some other servant of the pharaoh. I'm sure he's from Kush. He struggles with our languages and his accent is like nothing I've heard before."

Tombstone rubbed his unshaven jaw. "Ace, are

these *kekewe-saew* fellers the types to perform mystery rituals involving blood sacrifices an' screaming?"

Ace shrugged. "It seems plausible."

Gooper narrowed his eyes. "'Oo are the *kekewe-saew* loyal to? Thubis? Or Saret?"

Ace tapped her forehead with a finger. "Good question. Sam says the *kekewe-saew* are loyal to Prince Saret deep down. But they must obey direct commands from the pharaoh. That's Thubis at the moment."

Tombstone summarized, "Saret good but in prison. Thubis bad but in power. I'm with you so far. Did Sam explain th' ankhs an' the blood an' the screaming?"

"Morse code has its limits. We haven't chatted about those details. Sam mainly wants us to know that the Helm of Amun is very important. It's a legendary artifact of potent reputation. If Thubis wears the helm and is permitted to live by Amun, then Amun has given his blessing, and Thubis will be pharaoh. The same for Saret, of course."

Gooper said thoughtfully, "Not ter be a chump or anything, but is there any chance the story could be more lies? We 'aven't been told much truth so far this trip. Maybe it's Saret that's not legitimate, and Thubis that's the rightful ruler."

Ace's lips curved in a lopsided smile. "It's a possibility. And another good reason to gather information before acting."

Ace tensed. She held up a warning finger, eyes swiveling alertly.

She rose to her feet and whipped around the crate stacks almost before Gooper and Tombstone registered that she was gone. Ace halted almost immediately, face to face with Darby Entwhistle. "Oh! Good evening, Mr. Entwhistle. We, um, we make good time."

Entwhistle had dressed up his field jacket with a silky cravat. He emanated pungent whiffs of cologne. "Oh, quite! Quite. I do love a desert climate. It takes weather out of the equation and makes travel quite a pleasure. I wonder if you have a few moments to chat, Miss Carroway."

"I have a free calendar as far as I'm aware," said Ace, drily.

Ace and Darby strolled to the stern. As they did, Gooper and Tombstone crept around the opposite side of the crates to escape notice. They stopped after a few yards; they wanted to eavesdrop.

Darby sighed. "Miss Carroway, I've been going more than a bit mad these last few days."

"That doesn't sound good."

"When you were underwater so long, so very long, I was sure my throat would squeeze itself shut."

"I wasn't down long compared to the pearl divers of Polynesia …"

"No, Miss Carroway. You miss my point. Oh, goodness. I think I shall have to be very direct."

Ace's dark gold skin hues took on a richer, deeper color. She glanced at the sparkling waters of the Nile. Her shoulders tilted that way as if she was tempted to leap — to cool her hot face by diving in. "Um. Do you? You could continue to be oblique, honest."

"Americans are direct. Very blunt. You, yourself, have that admirable quality in abundance, Miss Carroway."

"I'm not exactly American. But I guess I can be

blunt."

"You're not American? But Dr. Fairweather said you were a fighter pilot in the Great War."

"That's true. But I have dual citizenship. India and the United States."

"Oh! Well, that would explain your lovely … erm. Oh, dear. Dear me, dear me." The British gentleman stopped gazing raptly at Ace's eyes and looked at his feet.

Ace's hot face did not cool, but there seemed no escape less drastic than leaping overboard.

Entwhistle blurted, "Miss Carroway, would you dine with me in Aswan?"

Ace hesitated. It was possible that she could pump Entwhistle for more information. It was also possible that she would learn nothing at cost of more lengthy, embarrassing conversation.

Entwhistle seized upon the tiny pause and spoke rapidly. "We should be at Aswan, shortly. We're in a hurry, but Dr. Fairweather agrees that a short stop won't hurt."

Ace's attempted smile faltered, never fully arriving on her face. "A *short* stop can't hurt."

"Oh, excellent! Thank you! I know a place famous for its kushari[3], but they also serve bangers and mash if that's more to your liking."

"Um. Wonderful."

"Oh, yes! Yes, indeed. It should be a treat after our Spartan rations. See you shortly, Miss Carroway. I do believe that I see the outskirts of town already."

---

[3] A dish with rice, macaroni, and lentils topped with spicy tomato sauce and garlic vinegar.

Ace mumbled an indistinct reply as Entwhistle moved forward toward the lounge.

Gooper and Tombstone crept back to the stern, finding Ace clutching the rail. The tendons on the backs of her hands rippled.

"Fellas," she whispered. "Did I ever say I appreciate you? Every time he said 'Dr. Fairweather' I wanted to knock his teeth in, the liar."

Tombstone touched the brim of his Stetson. "'Ppreciate ya back, ma'am."

Gooper crossed his bulging arms over his powerful chest. He fluffed his mustache out adamantly. "We're coming to dinner, too. Discreetly."

Ace snorted. "In Egypt, you two blend in about as well as a polar bear in Paris. Make it *very* discreetly. As in, the next restaurant over, maybe."

Gooper indicated Tombstone with a thumb. "I dunno. Tombstone blends in. 'E looks like a starving crocodile."

Tombstone squinted back. "An' you look like a hippo. A sunburned one."

112

CHAPTER 18

Twilight crept over the streets of Aswan. Gooper and Tombstone found it easy enough to remain undetected as they followed Entwhistle and Ace through the cooling buildings and tents. They kept far back. Entwhistle was tall. His brown tweed cap bobbed, alien above the brilliant fezzes, turbans, scarves, and head wrappings of the Aswan residents.

"Gooper," said Tombstone.

"Wot?"

"We ain't got no Egyptian money. We also ain't got no moony fork-tongue Brit gonna buy us dinner."

"Roight. No fine dining then."

Ace and her date disappeared through a door under a sign in Arabic characters with "'abyad kalb[4]" in small letters beneath. The phonetic translation left the bony cowboy and the muscular biologist as uninformed as before. They ambled as casually as possible around to the back of the place.

"I hope that the fact that about a hundred people been staring at us won't blow our cover," Tombstone muttered.

"We're safe. It's not a hundred, anyway. Eighty, maybe."

To their surprise and delight, the rear of the restaurant was an open patio surrounded by a low wall and

---

[4] White dog.

shrubs. They nuzzled into the shrubbery and spied.

Flies bit them. Spiky branches poked them. Delicious aromas made their mouths water.

And nothing happened. The scarred flyer in white shirt and pants sat straight-backed at a table for two with the tweed-coated Englishman. They ordered. They ate, mouthful by mouthful.

"Why're we here, again?" Tombstone whispered.

Gooper peered through leaves at the Texan. "We're bein' 'eroes."

"Yup. Noble an' gallant, that's us. Jes' like some moldy English romance novel. Notice the silent suffering? Dang flies."

Gooper's stomach rumbled.

"Shh!" Tombstone hissed.

Gooper opened his mouth to retort, but a glint caught his eye. He blinked toward Ace to see Entwhistle display for Ace a jeweled necklace. Silver and clusters of rubies sparkled in the candlelight.

"Blimey," he whispered.

"I'll be hornswaggled." Tombstone swallowed hard.

Ace sat ramrod straight. Her jaw muscles rippled. Negotiations dragged on for minutes with Entwhistle frozen in his pose of entreaty.

"Is she gonna take it?" Tombstone whispered.

"No idear. It looks more Frenchie than Egyptian. Wot's Darby doin' wif a flippin' Louis XIV necklace in the middle of the desert?"

"More mystery? I bet she takes it, then."

She took it.

And promptly stuffed it in her trouser pocket.

Chapter 19

Deep in the night, the little steamer left the still waters above the Aswan dam to struggle against the Nile's quickening currents. It also left the realm of electricity. No points of light graced the banks, but the thousands of stars overhead answered the challenge with glorious clarity.

In the abrupt loneliness an eerie quality descended. The banks of the Nile closed in and steepened, squeezing the river of light overhead to narrower limits. With the surface of the Nile no longer quiet, the deck heaved. Watery noises washed over the ceaseless throb of the turbines.

Bareem's eyes glinted in the dim light as three figures bore down on his favored lurking spot at the very rear of the boat. His teeth gleamed in a grimace as the outlines of Tombstone, Ace, and Gooper resolved.

"Pardon, mate. Could we 'ave privacy for a mo'?" Gooper said.

"Jes' a few minutes," Tombstone said. "This ship is jes' dang tiny."

Bareem's grimace transformed into a snarl. "You fools. You will soon see. You will soon wish you had listened to Bareem."

Ace said, gently, "We appreciate your warning, Bareem. Truly."

The bald man held his head high as he marched forward with deliberate steps.

"Huddle up," Ace said when the three were alone. "Tombstone, I need a match."

Tombstone obliged. Ace flicked the match head with a fingernail, and it flared to life. As the men half-expected, the purpose of the light was to inspect the necklace gift. They huddled close to gaze at its bejeweled complexity as Ace let it curl over her fingers.

Ace tossed the match off the stern. Silence reigned.

"You thinkin' what I'm thinkin'?" Tombstone said.

"Wot're you thinkin', then?"

There came the raspy sound of Tombstone's fingers scratching at his stubble. "I'm thinkin' this is stolen property."

"Aye. The Devonshire theft. That lady's Frenchie jewels."

Ace's voice strained as if she struggled against pain. "Agreed, though we can't prove it from what we read in the papers. Remember the story? The thieves entered through a high window. That sort of method sounds more like the *kekewe-saew* than Darby Entwhistle. They are said to be acrobats if you recall."

Tombstone groused, "Shore, but why steal jewelry in England and take it to south Egypt? I mean south Egypt, population zero."

Gooper snapped meaty fingers. "Kush. It's got ter 'ave summat to do wif Kush."

"But what?"

"No idea."

Ace heaved a long sigh. "Fellas, our only option is to play dumb, at least until we finally see Meroë-inet. I wouldn't say that if it weren't for Sam. He insists that we must rescue Prince Saret."

Gooper's teeth gleamed in the starlight. "Otherwise, we'd knock some 'eads together?"

"Otherwise, we'd absolutely knock some heads," Ace said.

"Dumb it is, then, m'lady."

"Dumb ain't no act fer Gooper."

"Ow, shut it, yew dessicated croc."

Ace said, "Fellas. Take the insults forward. Give me a diversion. I need to contact *Sky Arrow One* and then see if Sam can tell us more details."

"Wif pleasure, m'lady!"

Chapter 20

Dawn found the ship buried deep in a branching network of canyons. Over them was a deep azure cloudless sky, framed by towering cliffs of stone. A few circling vultures seemed the only wildlife in the bleak landscape.

"Miles" and Darby crowded the prow of the boat, scanning forward. In a quiet portion of water, they pointed to a flat rock on the west side of the canyon and called, "Stop there!" The helmsman reduced speed and nudged the boat over there.

The water around the flat rock was shallow, and the hull slid to rest on the sandy bottom. Unloading commenced. Ace, Tombstone, and Gooper worked alongside the Egyptian crew to transfer the crates from the ship to the flat rock using hand trucks and rollers. The large one that Ace and her associates knew contained Sam and four *kekewe-saew* came off last. It was heavy, but the crew pushed it with levers and it rolled off smoothly on its wheels.

Darby and "Miles" did no work. They wore holsters with pistols. Bareem stalked to a bare spot on the rock, folded his arms across his chest, and scowled.

Gooper nudged Tombstone and whispered, "I think 'is face is frozen that way."

After the unloading, Entwhistle doled out money to the Egyptian crew. It seemed like quite a lot of money. After the exchange, the steamer promptly pushed off.

It turned downriver and puttered away without a smile or wave. The party was left alone on the riverbank with a pile of crates.

Darby Entwhistle pointed to a crate. "We'll need that one first. Work on that one."

Ace, Gooper, and Tombstone set to work cracking it open with claw hammers. Inside, they discovered a set of four canoes. They unpacked the canoes and dragged them to the water's edge. They kept their mouths shut.

Darby and "Miles" watched the cruise boat disappear around the bend. When it was gone, "Miles" came to life. "Right. Let me just unlock that big one now." There was a row of padlocks on it, and he jingled a large key ring to find the keys to open them, one by one.

Ace, Gooper, and Tombstone found themselves unable to look away as the end of the crate creaked open on hinges. They caught a glimpse inside. Plush carpet covered the floor, tapestries decorated the walls, and bunk beds marched along near the ceiling. But their attention riveted to the parade of macabre creatures that scuttled out.

At first, the dark apparitions seemed more crab than human. They walked with legs splayed wide and hands raised in clawlike poses. Two men and two women wore black loincloths, and their heads were covered by god masks. Isis, Nephthys, Osiris, and Seth capered forth, moving with hypnotic oddness.

Gooper muttered, "Blimey. So them's the *kekewe-saew*."

Tombstone said, "Guess so." A moment later, he added, "Sam!"

It was true. Blinking a little in the light, Sam shuffled forth. The short, stout archaeologist wore shackles at wrists and ankles. He smiled wanly at Ace and his friends. After a moment, he hung his head.

"Sam?" Tombstone said worriedly.

Ace swiveled her gaze to Darby, or rather, down the barrel of the pistol he had drawn. Her voice dripped acid. "The big reveal, eh? You've been playing us like violins, haven't you?"

Darby sounded about the same as ever as he replied, but without any shred of shyness or subservience. His accents coarsened, less at home in university halls and more settled in city alleys. "It was necessary. But now let the veil of secrecy be raised! A word to the wise, don't do anything rash. We're just going to shackle you up. There's no use in trying to argue. You'll be prisoners for a little while. Not for long if you behave."

"Miles" ducked into the crate-apartment and returned carrying an armload of shackles. He continued where Darby left off. "We've still got a short journey to go. And these fellows, they're with us. So, behave."

"Yew lost me at 'shackle,'" Gooper growled.

"That goes double fer me." Tombstone's hands balled into bony fists.

The pair started moving, angling toward the shackles-carrying "Miles." They used crates and the cavorting *kekewe-saew* to keep out of the line of fire from Darby's pistol.

"No, my friends, do not," Sam pleaded.

Gooper stepped up to "Miles" and swung a left hook.

"Sheta neph!" barked Bareem.

The *kekewe-saew* paused in their dance-like movements to face Gooper and Tombstone. A smattering of air puff sounds blended with the sound of Gooper's heavy fist plastering "Miles." The expedition leader staggered back, reeling. He dropped manacles with a metallic clatter.

Gooper and Tombstone exchanged popeyed glances. Each plucked from the other's neck a small dart consisting of a thorn and a feather.

Sam shook his head. "Ah, friends. Brave friends. Good night."

Gooper and Tombstone collapsed bonelessly to the ground.

"Miles" rubbed his jaw and collected his scattered wits. "Told you they was a risk, Darby! Let's get to Kush before anything else happens."

Bareem spat on the ground. "Fools. Every one."

Ace said, "I'll go quietly." She hadn't moved much. In fact, all she had done during the diversion was to flick a switch on the small radio pulse unit tucked under her belt. Now, Ace herself emitted regular pulses of radio waves.

The *kekewe-saew* tilted their masks up, revealing serious, even mournful, faces. They were all about five feet tall, umber-skinned, and athletic in physique. Their ribs showed. Each god-mask had a built-in blowtube from which the poisoned darts flew.

The *kekewe-saew* slid the canoes in the water. "Miles" shackled Gooper and Tombstone at the wrists. With the help of the *kekewe-saew,* he dumped their limp bodies into canoes. Ace was made to paddle along with Bareem and some of the *kekewe-saew.* They paddled across the Nile toward a sheer cliff face.

Chapter 21

The entrance to Meroë-inet, the hidden valley of Kush, lay in plain sight yet completely invisible. It looked like a rocky fold in the canyon wall. Upon approach it transformed to a water-filled crack that curved in and around. The crease wound its way back into the side of the canyon. Ace could have touched both sides of the narrow opening by stretching out her hands, if her hands had been free. Instead, she dipped an oar in and out of the water, pushing into the unknown.

For many minutes, quiet swishings of paddles were the only sounds as they traversed the water-filled slot canyon. After an improbably long time, light glimmered in the forward direction. A wavy vertical crack of light appeared, shining blue-green. The stony walls flattened, smoothed to vertical perfection by human hands. They glided past rows of dark arrow slits. Ace caught glimpses of movement within. With a shiver, she realized that silent, vigilant guards had been observing them. They probably had arrows notched, ready to kill.

They emerged from the cliff through great carven gates ringed with battlements. At least a dozen spearmen stood, half-seen behind protective fortifications. A single songlike challenge rang out from a spearman. The *kekewe-saew* responded musically, and the canoes passed unmolested into sparkling sunlight.

Ace emerged on a lake at the bottom end of a fair,

wide valley. The valley was terraced and layered. The orchards and fields were deep green near lake level. The green faded to hues of amber and olive higher up until the high ridges reverted back to brown steppe. The water for irrigation all came from the lake, all lifted by muscle, either animal or human.

Across the lake and further up the valley, the outlines of monumental structures towered over the landscape. A palace or temple formed the pinnacle with a city billowing around it like a stony ball gown. People and animals moved in the distance.

Ace's heart soared at the majestic vision.

Nearer, at lake edge, women picked lemons in an orchard. They paused in their plucking to wave at the canoes. Ace thought the welcoming gesture a hopeful sign.

Posing like a dauntless explorer, Darby stood in the bow of the canoe, one leg planted high, his chest out. He grandly gestured to the new vista. "Welcome to Kush!"

The sight of him soured Ace's stomach.

Chapter 22

"What's your real name, Darby?" Ace asked between paddle strokes. The lake stretched over a mile long. They headed for the far end where the city proudly glittered.

"Eh?" Darby was jolted out of his conqueror's mood and turned to scowl at Ace. "It's Darby Entwhistle!"

Ace's steady, skeptical stare made Darby twitch.

He added, "Oh. Well. There is my brother. Bertram Entwhistle. He's been playing the part of Miles Fairweather."

"Why?" Ace inquired darkly.

Darby said righteously, "It was convenient for our dealings in Europe. No need for it now, of course."

"What happened to the real Miles Fairweather?"

Darby said in aggrieved tones, "Miss Carroway, what a suspicious mind you have! I'm a businessman, not a murderer. Fairweather is wherever Thubis wants him to be. Thubis is pharaoh here."

Ace felt her face heat. She resisted an urge to whack the smug off Darby's face with her paddle. Conscious of her growing anger, she inwardly recited a Wing Chun mantra. The ritual helped her accept her anger and calmed her heart rate. In clipped tones, she changed the subject to something less provocative. "Tell me about Kush."

"Isn't it lovely? The history involves something about Rameses II conquering a lot of Kush but not this part. And then the valley went secret and no one came in or out for centuries. Thus, a version of ancient Egyptian and Kushite culture remained. The natives like to say 'Meroë-inet,' meaning the hidden valley of Meroë, another name for Kush."

"What happens next?"

Darby practically purred. "We're V.I.P.s, Miss Carroway. Very important persons. We're going straight to the pharaoh, and we won't be kept waiting. There will be a short business negotiation. The language barrier isn't that serious. There are some scholar-priests who know bits of Arabic and English. I'm looking forward to this!"

"Why?"

"You'll see. You'll see."

The canoes reached stone docks at the city end of the lake. Cleanly-carved stonework dominated the architecture. Freestanding columns were covered in hieroglyphs and stylized reliefs. Long cascades of stairs flowed through the campus. No city tower rose higher than the imposing palatial structure that formed the apex of the city. Colorful sculpture met the eye along every sightline in perfect repair and painted marvelously. The human carvings had realistic skin tone pigments spiced with bright decorations. Beaten and polished gold appeared frequently, taking the place of paint.

"Oh!" Sam's gasp of wonder escaped his lips unbidden, audible to all.

The architecture stunned. People dressed exactly like the sculptures and paintings that adorned the streets went about their business. It was as if the art-work had come alive to re-create ancient Egypt. Men wore *shendyts*, wrapped skirts with belts and pleated fronts. Women dressed in *kalasiris*, simple sheath dresses.

In contrast to the friendly waves from the lemon harvesters, the reception party at the dock was stoic. Twenty sober warriors held spears or kept their hands on the hilts of sheathed *khopesh* curved swords. The warriors glittered in spotlessly clean shendyts and shiny bronze armbands and bracers. Most wore bronze caps with single feathers, but the one wearing a full head-dress spoke a few rapid words. Ace did not understand the speech, but she heard echoes of Bareem's accent in it.

Some warriors tumbled the unconscious Gooper and Tombstone into two-poled litters and carried them. Darby and his brother Bertram, who still rubbed at his jaw, led the way. They carried a chest between them: a bound box about the size of a grocery bag. Sam and Ace walked behind them, each flanked by warriors. The group of *kekewe-saew* came last, and they came in formation, two by two, stepping like ballet dancers.

Ascending three flights of steps, they passed near a stone erection that resembled a sarsen circle monu-ment. Its shape eerily echoed Stonehenge, but it was engineered geometrically neater and more precise. Some patient sculptor had carved mythological reliefs into each trilithon. Both Ace and Sam stared at it as they slowly passed, thinking of midnight screams and splattered blood.

They trudged up three more flights of steps. The warriors carrying Gooper and Tombstone split off from the main party. They disappeared from sight through a stone doorway marked with a shepherd's crook.

Ace whispered worriedly to Sam, "Do you know where they are being taken?"

"The royal dungeons," he answered promptly.

As they climbed the final wide staircases, awe set in. The columns grew larger and higher, and the statues depicting gods or pharaohs towered into unbelief. Framed in this majesty was the pharaoh, seated with crook scepter and headdress. His ornate throne ascended even higher on a three-step stone dais, surrounded by scribes and servants. His eyes bulged out, cold, arrogant, and uncaring.

Warriors pressed downward on Sam's and Ace's shoulders and kicked at the backs of their knees. They folded to a kneel, joining in subservience the rest of the warriors and the rows of *kekewe-saew* too. Ace's face grimaced in pain and her face flushed in humiliation.

"Greetings, o Thubis, pharaoh of Meroë-inet!" Darby and Bertram bowed, holding a hand over their hearts.

Bareem had also prostrated himself, but as the English rang out, he stood and spoke to the Pharaoh. The Pharaoh spoke, and Bareem spoke to the Englishmen. "The Pharaoh acknowledges. The Pharaoh would receive his gift."

"We hope the great Pharaoh looks with kindness

upon his humble servants. We return to his possession the Helm of Amun!" Darby had Bertram hold the box, and he opened it. Darby lifted out a flat-topped crown in the Egyptian style apparently made of solid gold inlaid with rubies. Though, of course, it must be hollow.

Thubis rose. His thirsting eyes stared at the helm as if it was an oasis. He spoke rapidly and waddled forward to lift the helm from its box. Bareem translated, "The Pharaoh acknowledges. The Pharaoh grants one household to the English brothers and six servants. The Pharaoh may grant one more wish."

"Rank equal to a high priest if it pleases the Pharaoh." Darby's ready answer tripped from his tongue. Bareem's eyes grew noticeably wider, then narrowed to his normal contemptuous expression. He repeated the request to the Pharaoh. Thubis grew an expression of distaste on his cruel features and eyed the brothers for a few moments before nodding yes and saying, "Ce!"

Ace saw tension melt from Darby's shoulders. Darby bowed again. "The Pharaoh is most wise and most generous. After his coronation, perhaps we can speak of gemstones." Darby produced from a pocket a large, cut specimen of purple amethyst. He handed it to Bareem who held it in his open palm as if afraid the semi-precious quartz variant would bite him.

A glint of avid desire sparked in the Pharaoh's bulging eyes. Darby and Bertram backed away. Thubis spoke with Bareem. The interpreter handed Thubis the amethyst and then spoke to the Englishmen. "The great Thubis, Pharaoh of Meroë-inet, bids you to take the house of High Priest Hut-Met."

A highly-decorated man nearby started, his gold

jewelry jingling. His shocked face gradually turned mournful, and his chin wobbled as if he held back tears. It was an easy guess that the poor fellow was High Priest Hut-Met.

Darby bowed. "As Pharaoh says, so shall it be. One last trifle. These foreigners. I want them as slaves."

Sam and Ace both twitched, then tried to stand. The warriors surrounding them had other ideas. With rough hands laid upon their shoulders and necks the warriors kept the pair on their knees. There was more speaking in the language of Kush, and then the interpreter said, "So shall it be. Now, go." Bareem spoke to High Priest Hut-Met. The trembling former high priest nodded and led the way, and they left the august presence of the pharaoh.

Chapter 23

The party wound through paved streets. Hut-Met, Ace and Sam, and the Entwhistle brothers. They passed through the proud shadows of paintings, sculptures, and banners. Citizens looked at them with curiosity.

The castes were obvious at a glance. The richest class wore dazzling bangles, gold collars, varied head ornaments. They wore shendyts or kalasiri so long they restricted the ankles and impeded walking. The working-class wore practical headdresses and knee-length skirts. Copper ornaments decorated their foreheads, ear lobes, necks, and wrists. The servant class carved ornaments from wood or wove them from fiber. Only hair adorned their heads. The men wore loincloths and the women thigh-length kalasiris.

One mischievous upper-caste boy pinched the hem of Darby's safari jacket, making fun of the outlandish costume. Darby cuffed the imp, who wailed. High priest Hut-Met reprimanded the boy until his cries subsided to wide-eyed snuffles. The boy stared at the strangers, especially the pair of white-skinned high priests.

The procession exited the city. Stone-paved streets became dirt roads. Centuries of pounding footfalls, plodding hoofs, and rolling cart wheels had powdered the dirt into dust and raised little roadside embankments.

Ace had been stewing as they trekked. Even her wing chun mantras did little to cool the heat of her emotions. Finally, she shot a glare over her shoulder at Darby. "You'd better explain what you meant by 'I want them as slaves,' Entwhistle."

A hurt expression wiped away Darby's smug. "Miss Carroway, it is merely the language they speak. You'll find no actual slavery, here. Only the servant caste."

Ace halted, causing Bertram to halt — and also unholster his pistol. She spoke through clenched teeth at Darby. "I'm not going to take orders, Entwhistle."

"Calm, Miss Carroway. I assure you that you mean far more to me than that. I respect you deeply. Soon, indeed almost instantly if you desire it, you will have an entire household at your command."

"What's your plan?"

Bertram poked his gun between Ace's shoulder blades. He still looked like a baker, but his voice growled like a cheap thug. "Keep walking. Darby — or should I say Romeo? — tell her your *plan*."

Darby's chin jutted forward. After a fleeting glance at Ace's fiery eyes, he studied Sam's back instead. "I have already stated my affection for you, Miss Carroway. This is merely the continuation of it. I will have you at my side. I *will*."

"I have something to say about that!" Ace spat.

"Please don't be so angry, Miss Carroway. I'm only being practical."

"You're being infuriating. I don't remember a time I was this angry." Ace jammed a hand into her trouser pocket.

Bertram snapped, "Watch it!"

"Calm down. It's just this." The flyer's saccharine

tones seemed soothing on the surface, even if they sounded like strangling in progress underneath. A Louis XIV diamond necklace glittered, draped over her knuckles.

Hut-Met happened to glance back. His eyes popped and he gasped. Attentive Sam's fists clenched.

Darby began, "Miss Carroway …"

Ace tossed the diamonds in a high arc. As the twinkling missile spun through the air, she bit off two words. "Courtship's over."

Darby bleated, "My necklace!" He pivoted and chased the jewels. Bertram held steady, his gun still aiming through Ace's belly.

"Not yours. It belongs to an old woman in Devonshire. Thief." Ace faced away from the pistol and marched forward after Hut-Met.

Hut-Met watched Darby scoop the necklace up out of the dust, then heaved a sigh. He resumed the trek at a plodding pace.

When Darby caught up with the procession, Bertram said, "You're an idiot."

Darby flushed. "Shut it, you. I'm a good businessman." He dusted off the necklace and stowed it in his own pocket. "Miss Carroway, I'm sure you'll see it my way soon enough. Let's push on, shall we?"

No one replied.

With feet that dragged and hesitated, Hut-Met led Ace, Sam, and the Englishmen to a spacious villa surrounded by barley fields. It lay a half-mile north of the temple complex about halfway up the valley slope. Cheerful paint adorned the architecture, more for beauty's sake than to pay homage to the pantheon of gods. Open air rooms encircled a courtyard, with walls to fill in the gaps. The Englishmen ordered Ace and Sam to idle in the center of the garden courtyard in plain sight. Darby and Bertram inspected their new home at a smiling stroll. They patted their holstered pistols from time to time, with significant glances to Ace and Sam.

Hut-Met tearfully broke the news to his wife, three children, and four servants. As the pair of smug Englishmen strolled, the family packed their belongings into hand carts.

Sam and Ace conversed in whispers.

"I am sorry, Lady Ace. I feel as if I have given exactly the wrong advice."

"It's not so bad, Sam. This hidden valley boggles the mind! I saw you staring too. You're as amazed as I am."

"I am indeed walking as if in a dream," Sam said wistfully. He tapped his chin. "Memsahib, did you happen to read the book I wrote on the Coptic language?"

"Yes, actually. I found it captivating. You made the point that Coptic is the clearest window we have on the language of ancient Egypt. I still couldn't understand the guards or the pharaoh though."

"I can help with comprehension, Lady Ace. The order of nouns and adjectives is reversed from Coptic. Pronunciations have transformed, but the words are largely intact. Here, let me illustrate." Sam spent the next fifteen minutes sharing his insights into the spoken language. He had not been idle during his time with the *kekewe-saew*.

Ace absorbed his instruction attentively. The strident voices of Hut-Met's children floated over the adobe walls of the villa. Ace listened, then asked, "Did the brother complain about having to share a room with the sister?"

"Yes, Lady Ace! You have understood! I am amazed you remember Coptic so well."

"I was interested. It was your work." Ace scanned around for eavesdroppers, but the Entwhistle brothers were occupied. "Now. On to Gooper and Tombstone. You were poisoned by darts too, I gather?"

"Yes, memsahib. I was marked for kidnapping at the order of Darby Entwhistle."

Ace blinked. "But Darby blamed the kekewe-saew, according to Tombstone."

"Memsahib, I fear the Darby Enwhistle is not a stickler with the truth."

Ace grimaced. "You can say that again. So why did he want you captured?"

"I think he feared I was closer to finding out his scheme than I was. The *kekewe-saew,* the *guardians of darkness*, they easily trapped me. They put me to sleep and I woke up inside the small apartment that resembles a shipping crate on the outside."

"Are you all right, after having been trapped inside for so long?"

Sam replied placidly, "Oh, yes, Lady Ace. We emerged to stretch our legs and take baths several times. London. Genoa. Cairo. Aswan. I do admit that the cuisine became tedious. Biscuits, mostly."

"Poor Sam. But I'm so glad you're alive! We worried so. The blood. All the blood. Do you know, Sam? Why the splashes of animal blood?"

"A ritual sacrifice, memsahib. They honor a different god in the pantheon each week. It is normally done weekly, but the *kekewe-saew* felt a need to catch up on time lost during travel. They came to England inside the large crate, too."

"And the midnight scream?"

"Excellent acting, memsahib. One of the *kekewe-saew* plays the part of a mortal soul leaving the material world to enter the afterlife. The *kekewe-saew* are avatars of Nephthys, goddess of death."

"It left a vivid impression," Ace murmured. "Tell me what Darby's scheme is."

"His whole scheme, perhaps I do not know. But his trip to England was to collect firstly the Helm of Amun and secondly jewels. The Helm of Amun was to crown the Pharaoh as you have seen. I am not sure of the significance of the jewels."

"Jewels? I have a guess. Gold seems plentiful here, but even the upper caste wear only colored minerals like malachite or corroded copper. I have seen no rubies or sapphires or anything we might call precious stones. I think jewels have great value. Darby and his brother are planning to turn a profit, I guess. Gold may be cheap in Meroë-inet, but they know it is expensive outside the hidden valley. And the reverse is true for gemstones."

"They play games with us all, Lady Ace," said Sam mournfully. "They pull the strings, and we dance like puppets."

Ace chewed on her lower lip. "I suppose they do, but they also play with fire. This valley seems a throwback to ancient Egypt. But that means a lot more than hieroglyphs, statues, and yesterday's fashion. The rigid caste system means that life is cheap, that slavery is a way of life, and that the pharaoh is seen as a god walking in mortal form."

"His word is law. Yes."

"Sam, I didn't have time to mention this to anyone, but the airship is meeting me tonight at midnight."

"You brought an airship? How is this possible?"

"Our pulse transmitters, Sam. We've been in contact all along."

"But whose airship is it?"

Giggles burbled up Ace's throat unbidden. "It's mine! *Sky Arrow One.*" Her grin faded. "Sam, I will need to leave this house to track down Gooper and Tombstone. That will presumably trigger some sort of hunt for me. Would you be willing to stay here and not try to escape for a day or two? That way, I'll know where you are when I come back."

"Yes, Lady Ace, I will stay. I will learn what I can as I am made to do menial tasks for the benefit of men I despise."

"Sam. Your sense of humor is as dry as the desert out there."

The pair quieted when the Entwhistle brothers came to observe the departure of Hut-Met and his household. The family dragged themselves away, sending ugly glares to the pair. At the last minute Hut-Met's wife whirled and shook her fist at them. Out burst an angry staccato of verbiage.

Ace tried to decode the language and, after a moment of deep concentration, winced. "Oh, my! If that was anatomically possible, it would be very painful."

Sam chuckled.

CHAPTER 24

The Englishmen conferred, and Ace heard snatches of their words. "… servants … market … buy …"

Then Bertram left, following Hut-Met toward the city. Darby sauntered toward Ace and Sam. "Life is good and about to get better," he announced. "This is a fine house. Lovely view. Plenty of space. Bertram's just off to see if he can get a cook and some domestic help." He bounced on the balls of his feet, smiling.

Ace rose to her feet.

Darby took a step back, putting a hand on his holster. He scolded, "Don't get any hasty Yankee ideas, Miss Carroway. There's no escaping the valley. No one gets out, not unless the pharaoh orders it. Perhaps you didn't see the rows and rows of little vertical windows at the little canyon that goes to the Nile. Well, they're full of archers. So don't try that way, unless you want to play reverse hedgehog. Don't try climbing out of the valley either. The desert is vast, and the pharaoh's chariots are swift!" Darby's mood lifted as he enjoyed his own eloquence.

Sam struggled to his feet, too, though he still wore shackles, unlike Ace.

Ace said, evenly, "What's going to happen next?"

Darby preened and made a show of bringing out his pipe and pressing tobacco into the bowl. "Nothing much is what happens next. It's time to slow down and enjoy the good life. Miss Carroway, I just negotiated a rank above *everyone*. Everyone except a handful of high priests and the god-king himself! If Bertram or I issue an order, we will be *obeyed!* I have *arrived*, Miss Carroway. I'm retired! I'm out of a job and set for life! And so young! Ha! Ha!"

Ace's dark face did not share in the mirth.

Entwhistle's smile faded. "Miss Carroway, this is the time for you to accept facts. This is the time for you to start working the system for your own benefit. Who is in charge? I am! But I have strings, and they can be pulled. I'm ever so malleable, trust me."

"What about Gooper and Tombstone?"

"Pff. I don't know. They'll be fine. They'll probably be put to work like everyone else. Everyone except those of High Priest caste! Ha! We get to give orders, not take them." Darby laughed merrily, then broke off. He stabbed a finger at Sam. "You! See that pump over there? Start filling the basin with water."

Sam stoically regarded Darby. He glanced at Ace. He nodded to Darby. "Yes, sahib." Sam trudged off to start drawing water.

Ace pinched the bridge of her nose with thumb and forefinger as if suffering from a headache.

Darby watched Sam leave. He stepped toward Ace. He spoke with soft persuasion, "Think about it. Whatever you desire can be had. Servants, gold, the finest clothes, the most exquisite cuisine. All you need is a little bit of patience. Don't fight it. Simply enjoy yourself. Work with me, Ace Carroway, and you'll live like a queen. You'll almost *be* a queen!"

Ace leveled a steady gaze at him. "Darby."

"Yes, Miss Carroway?" Darby smiled most handsomely.

"Shut up."

Darby blinked.

In a movement almost too quick for the eye, Ace shot out her right hand and dug it into his neck, squeezing his carotid artery.

Darby gasped, his open mouth pulsing like a fish. His brain began fogging immediately, but in a moment of lucidity, Darby fumbled for his gun.

But Ace had already removed it from its holster. She showed it to him as he struggled, his vision blurring around the edges. Darby flailed, but his movements grew weak. He sank to his knees. Ace laid him down backward, maintaining the pressure on his neck for a long time. "You deserve *so* much worse, you delusional egotist." Solicitously, she returned his gun to his holster.

"I think Mr. Entwhistle might be waking with a headache," Sam observed, reaching to twirl his mustache in satisfaction.

Ace replied in businesslike tones, "I'm going to go scrounge clothes that will blend in. Then, I'll see about Gooper and Tombstone. I remember the doorway they disappeared into."

"Yes, memsahib."

"Sam, I'd like you to play the dutiful servant. Learn all you can, please. Especially about Prince Saret."

"Oh, indubitably. This I will do. Lady Ace? Before you go, look! This water pump is an Archimedes screw. Fascinating, yes?"

After marveling at the pump's timeless physics and artful construction, Ace plundered the back rooms of the villa. She reappeared dressed in a short kalasiri with necklaces and bangles made of bundles of barley stalks and wood. She squinted at the sun. "An hour of light left. I'm sorry you might miss a bit of action, Sam, but it won't be long, and we desperately need to know more about the local politics."

"I understand perfectly, Lady Ace." Sam waved in farewell.

With her trousers and shirt stuffed into her boots and tucked under an arm, she jogged off.

Sam murmured to himself, "Dressed as the most lowly of servants, yet she walks as proudly as royalty."

Then he amused himself by pumping enormous amounts of water. Orders were orders, after all. He failed entirely to help Darby as the Englishman painfully regained consciousness.

Chapter 25

Tombstone came to and groggily pried his eyes open. Compared to eyes-closed, it wasn't much lighter.

"'Ere 'e is now. Tombstone? You awake?" It was Gooper's familiar Cockney rumble.

"Uh. I reckon," Tombstone said past sluggish lips.

A new voice, mature in upper crust British, said, "Welcome back to the land of the barely living. Also, thank you. We hadn't been fed in quite a while, but they tossed food in here when you came. I'm Miles Fairweather. That's Prince Saret."

Tombstone blinked furiously, then stared around in the gloom. The only light came from distant torchlight that filtered through a high hole in the wall. Tombstone could make out four walls and three shadowy forms. Fuzzily, he did the accounting. Gooper, Fairweather, and Saret added up to three. Check.

"I'm Tombstone. Where th' Sam Hill are we?"

"It's a dungeon, Tombstone. But don't yew worry. Yer comin' up in the world. This is no ordinary dungeon. This is the royal dungeon." Gooper informed him.

"Oh, haw, haw," Tombstone grumbled.

"Well met," said Prince Saret in halting English. He sounded like a young man.

Tombstone shook cobwebs out of his head. "Wait. Prince Saret. It's all comin' back, now. You were the rightful heir to th' throne or somethin' like that, but somehow you got in prison instead."

Miles Fairweather replied, "That's the long and short of it, yes. Thubis was in the High Priest caste. He bloody well should've stayed there given that Saret was the legitimate heir. Those blasted Entwhistle brothers put the idea in his head. I wish I'd never clapped eyes on—" A grunt of pain choked off his voice.

"Miles. Hurt," said Prince Saret.

"You can say that again!" Miles agreed weakly, wheezing. "It comes and goes, but when it comes, it's not pleasant."

"Aw, shucks. Well. We're in quite a pickle. That's fer sure. I suppose there's no escape, huh?" Tombstone drawled dolefully.

"No escape, no. But a guard comes every day. Well. Most days," Miles said, wearily.

They were alone in the bare room. There wasn't even a bed. Tombstone patted himself down. "Shewt. No belt. No knife. No boots. They even took mah hat."

Over the next few hours, Gooper and Tombstone explored the cell, looking for anything that might turn into an escape plan. Rack their brains as they might, they came up empty. The door, perhaps, should have been the weak point, but it was constructed of solid copper, heavy and thick. Everyone sat on the ground.

Fairweather suffered sharp abdominal pains every few minutes. A sheen of sweat glistened on his face. Saret waved a hand to indicate the archaeologist. "Hurt. Less hurt yesterday. More hurt today."

"Shewt," Tombstone said. "Wish Ace were here. She's a doctor."

"Ace," Saret repeated. He spoke a string of words

in his native tongue. Fairweather answered in the same language.

Gooper sniffed contemptuously. "Yew bony skeleton. Don't be daft. Surely, she's locked up somewhere, too. An' if not, 'ow would she know where to find us? Naw, our goose is cooked. Almost as cooked as poor Fairweather, 'ere."

Tombstone sounded as mournful as the undertaker he resembled. "I guess you're right, pardner. We're as good as dead."

A sharp metallic clank made them jump. The solid copper door moved. Dirt sifted down from the doorframe.

Fairweather muttered, "Who is it? The guards already came today."

The door swung open all the way. The torchlit silhouette was instantly recognizable to Gooper and Tombstone. "Ace!" they said simultaneously.

Ace spoke quietly and crisply. "Well, hello. Thanks for talking. I homed in on that right away."

"Erm, don't mention it," Gooper said.

"Gracious, it's dark in here. Are you alone?"

Saret emerged from around Gooper's bulk. "Woman," he said in halting English.

Tombstone said, "That there's Prince Saret."

Gooper added, "And we've got Miles Fairweather, too. The *real* Miles Fairweather."

"Greetings, milady," Fairweather said through a hoarse throat.

"What a pleasant surprise! Greetings, Re-pat Saret. Hello, Doctor Fairweather. Glad to find you both alive. Well, come on, everybody." Ace beckoned as she backed away into a torchlit stone passage. The four prisoners followed, blinking as their eyes adjusted to the light.

Ace knelt over the crumpled form of a jailor and checked his neck pulse. She murmured over her shoulder, "Outside, it's early evening. There were two guards, but I persuaded them to nap. Once outside on the street, we need to head north."

"This is unbelievable!" Fairweather grinned broadly from a sand-colored nest of about a month's beard growth.

Saret stared at Ace and spoke a string of syllables, ending in, "Isis."

Tombstone grew a skeleton grin and shook his head. "Ace, not Isis."

Gooper and Tombstone were barefoot and stripped down to trousers and shirts. Fairweather and Saret were also barefoot and dressed in rags. Ace's associates were in the pink of health, but Fairweather and Saret were haggard and grim. They shuffled after Ace down a row of copper doors.

Saret passed the first, then halted. Stepping back, he pulled at the bronze bar that locked the door. It slid, and he pushed at the door. He spoke a syllable into the blackness within, then moved on to the next.

Gooper remarked, "What a thoughtful bloke! This 'ere dungeon is cruel. Too 'orrid for even a murderer."

Tombstone squinted. "Saret's got somethin' wrong with his right hand. Missin' a couple fingers." Saret's grievous injury was fully healed. His pinkie and ring finger were gone all the way to the wrist, making his right hand oddly slender. Saret did not favor it, and used it with firm purpose as he opened cell door after cell door.

Before they reached the end of the row of cells, pain struck Miles. He stifled a cry and sagged against the side of the passage.

In an instant, Ace whisked back and examined the weather-beaten explorer. Miles sweated more profusely than before. He hoarsely whispered, "It's getting worse. The pain is more steady now."

"Does this hurt?" Ace pressed on the right side of his abdomen.

"Ghhhkkkk!" gasped Fairweather. He doubled over in agony.

Ace straightened and pointed to Gooper and Tombstone. "You two, take his arms and help him. It's acute appendicitis. Unfortunately, we can't rest. We have to get out of town before the alarm is raised." Ace glanced at Saret and spoke a sentence that sounded completely alien to Gooper and Tombstone. Saret flashed a tight grin and spoke back in the same language.

"Appendicitis?" Fairweather passed a hand over his sweat-shined brow.

Ace switched to English. "Saret will lead us out. Dr. Fairweather, I will simply ask you to try to keep quiet, no matter the agony. The quickest help for you will be the airship."

Saret opened the last door in the hall, then squared off to face Ace. He had to look up at the tall woman to meet her eyes. They exchanged measuring glances, gold meeting soft brown. The mutual sizing-up ended in small smiles.

A few ragged prisoners ventured out of their cells like century sleepers seeing dawn for the first time in generations. The Carroway party set off at the fastest pace Fairweather could manage.

Stairs led up through a heavy door and into a guardroom in which Ace's second victim sprawled. The exit from there led to the city's main way, lit here and there by oil lamps. In her servant's garb, only Ace could pass as normally-dressed if they were seen in good light. A few shadow-wrapped townspeople travelled up and down the complicated criss-crossings of stairways and avenues. Quiet reigned. Faintly, the songs of insects trilled in the night air. The stars gleamed overhead.

Boldly, Saret led them on. They angled away from the palace and center of town. He pointed toward an intersection ahead. It was lit by a flickering lamp, but that light seemed to be the last one between them and the darkness of lesser streets.

Onward they toiled. Fairweather hung between Tombstone and Gooper. Ace kept a rear guard. At the intersection, they passed under the lamp's bracket.

And Saret stopped short, almost colliding with a citizen of the city.

She wore gold on her wrists and forehead, and she stared at Saret as the deposed prince gazed back.

Ace understood Saret as he spoke in the tongue of Kush. "Do you hope for the return of Saret, sister?"

Her hand flew to her open mouth, her eyes widening even more. She nodded.

Saret murmured, "Hope lives on. Tell them only that." The tableau broke. The woman stepped aside and watched the party slide away into darker streets.

Just then in the city, bells clanged, deep and brassy. The metallic vibrations reverberated. In the cool desert air, the sounds would travel for miles.

Saret spoke two words to Ace.

Ace translated. "It is the alarm bell. Our escape is known."

Chapter 26

The party kept hustling forward along alleys and staircases that ascended the sides of the valley. They had left blocky buildings behind, in favor of smaller apartments. Citizens emerged to turn curious faces toward the city center. No one hailed the ragged party and they passed through one last walled section of the road to exit the city. Fairweather moaned deliriously from time to time, but there seemed no one to hear now.

Except that Ace became more and more convinced that there *was*. The hackles on the back of her neck would not settle. From time to time, she thought she heard more than the echo of their own footsteps, but when she tried to pierce the gloom behind her, only stillness met her vision.

The skin between Ace's shoulder blades itched, as if anticipating an arrow to whisk through the darkness and bury itself there. Ace strained her ears to the limits of her training. Between the shuffling of bare feet and the heavy breathing of the party, she heard the muted patter of many footsteps. But the footfalls came from up ahead, not behind.

Ace whisked to the front of the little group and wordlessly mimed, lightly pushing on Saret, Gooper, and Tombstone. The men got the hint and tiptoed off the road.

Soon they all heard the shuffling of sandaled feet

on the road, which by now was no paved city thoroughfare but a lane of beaten, compacted dirt. They all hunkered down and went motionless. The night was dark, but there was no cover. Whoever was coming would pass ten feet away.

Those on the road all carried spears. The starlight glinted off the bronze-bladed weapons. There seemed to be four of them, and they loped along at a jog.

For a moment, it appeared as if they would sail right by the fugitives, but the last warrior caught a glimpse and slowed down. He spoke a few words. The words sounded like a challenge.

Miles Fairweather spasmed, squirming in agony.

Saret answered the challenge, his voice calm and soothing.

Whatever he said seemed to satisfy the guard who grunted softly, then ran to join the rest of his party as they hurried toward the city.

Miles Fairweather's agony eased, and he panted. They listened to his labored breathing and the receding footsteps of the warriors.

"Wot'd they say?" Gooper finally asked.

"The spearman wanted to know what the alarm bells were about. Saret told them that they should go find out," Ace replied. She spoke a few Kush words to Saret, who chuckled.

Saret's eager feet outpaced the rest, and from time to time he paused to wait, only to spring away once they arrived. Ace held to the rear spot, her sixth sense still fraying her nerves. But whatever shadows plagued her mind, they did not materialize into physical form. The remainder of the lonely journey stretched almost too long for Miles Fairweather. Gooper and Tombstone all but carried the poor fellow. After a nightmarish eternity for him, they arrived at a country villa with flickering lamplight visible in its windows. Saret raced to the front door and called, "Khontum! Khontum!"

There was a brief silence, and then a female voice called, "Saret?"

The door opened, and the silhouette of a woman blocked the faint lamp light from inside. "Saret!" she cried, her voice thickened by emotion. The pair threw arms around each other and Saret repeated, "Khontum! Khontum!" over and over as they embraced.

"Aww!" Gooper sighed, "Now that's an 'appy sight!"

Ace took his word for it. She probed the darkness behind her with intent eyes. She muttered, "I feel like we are being followed, but I hear the airship already. We should show a torch so they know where to land."

"Airship? Hot diggety!"

Ace spoke to the clinging couple in Kush. Saret and Khontum disappeared into the house as a unit. They returned with a stick wrapped with linen and brightly afire. By then, the drone of the airship's engines was obvious to all.

Soon, its gigantic shape blotted out the stars as it carefully descended. Ace guided it in with sweeps of the linen torch. Electric torches speared downwards, playing here and there. Ropes dropped, and Tombstone and Gooper leapt into action, guiding the airship to a gentle landing. The engines cut out. Compressors whirred, reducing lift. *Sky Arrow One* had arrived.

Saret and Khontum stayed inseparable. As one, they watched the landing with round eyes.

Ace, however, had little time for romance. "Get Fairweather into the gondola, please. We'll use the back of the lounge as an infirmary. Tombstone, you'll be in charge of anesthesia. I'll show you how." And, in softer tones, "You'll be fine, Dr. Fairweather. We caught it in time and we have surgery supplies in the airship."

"I'm just about all in," wheezed Fairweather.

Ace requested water of Saret and Khontum. "Eioue." They nodded and disappeared into their house.

Vivian and Gilbert lowered the stairs, then backed up in surprise. Barefoot and half-dressed, Gooper and Tombstone dragged in a writhing and moaning fellow dressed even worse. Ace followed and directed the clearing of a table. Joyce Harcourt emerged from the cockpit and blinked at the sight. "What, now?"

Tombstone said, "This is Miles Fairweather, ma'am. He's about to have his appendix out," said Tombstone.

Ace talked while unpacking instruments from a case she pulled from a cubby hole. In particular, she had a device consisting of a breath mask and squeeze bulb. "Hello, everybody. Sorry for the rush, but time is of the essence. Vivian, fetch a clean sheet and cut a hole in it about the size of a basketball. Gooper, get his shirt off, then clean him gently. With water first, then alcohol. Tombstone, come here. This breath mask with the squeeze bulb is your responsibility. The chloroform goes in a pad here, and you control the amount he breathes here. At all times his heart must beat strongly, so you'll be concentrating hard on his pulse and breathing. You'll ignore everything else. Clear?"

Ace poured chloroform onto a cotton pad and tucked that into the breathing mask device. She came to Fairweather's head and met his pain-filled eyes. "You'll go to sleep now, Dr. Fairweather. It'll be a relief, I'm sure."

"Quite. Carry on," the archaeologist said with a clench-jawed smile. Ace and Tombstone put the breath mask on him, and Tombstone regularly squeezed the bulb.

Saret and Khontum arrived, bearing a large amphora brimming with water. Seen in the lounge's electric light, Khontum's painted eyes and gold ornaments sparkled. But she had eyes only for the dirt-smeared, ragged young man glued to her side. For his part, Saret drank in the sight of her like a man dying of thirst. Khontum drew rapt stares from the airship's occupants, too, as they experienced their first taste of the wonders of Meroë-inet. The elegant drapes of her flowing kalasiri and belt ties nearly brushed the ground. Gold sparkled in her wide, circular collar. The young woman had steady, wise eyes and a dimple in her chin.

Ace snapped them out of it. "Gilbert and Vivian, close the gondola door and lock it. I can't shake the feeling we were followed. Gooper? Saret and Khontum brought fresh water. Get to cleaning. Gently."

Ace used some of the water to wash her hands and Gooper used more to clean Fairweather's skin. They cleaned again using alcohol and cotton swabs, then

Ace arranged the sheet with the hole over Fairweather's bare belly.

Everyone stayed to watch the surgery, even Vivian and Gilbert. They both paled when Ace selected a scalpel from her case and unhesitatingly sliced an incision in Fairweather's abdomen. They glanced at each other and mouthed, "Wow!"

From Ace's perspective, the surgery was very satisfying and quick. She didn't nick any arteries, and her first guess on the location of the swollen appendix proved correct. She soon removed it. As Ace plopped the swollen organelle into a jar, Gilbert abruptly sat down. Vivian fanned him. Ace sutured her incision closed. She directed Tombstone to gradually end the chloroform and gave Fairweather an injection.

Chapter 27

Two hours before dawn, the surgery cleanup was over. They all sat around in the gondola's lounge and sipped coffee except for a sleeping, blanket-bundled Fairweather. Even Saret and Khontum tried the coffee, laughing at its alien taste.

Ace reflected, "Four of us are escaped prisoners. I should assume that I'm a criminal too, though Darby might not admit to anyone that I'm gone. I think we should simply fly away during daylight hours. We can come back in the night and see what Sam has learned. We'll need to decide on what we can do to help Prince Saret as well."

Ace tilted her head to one side and swiveled her eyes to Joyce Harcourt. "But first, a tale from the aeronauts! You found me just fine. I suppose you homed in on my pulse transmitter?"

"Yes, Ace, that's right." Joyce tapped her temple with a finger. "Except that we tracked our way to the suitcase transmitter first. It was just … sitting there on a flat rock down in the canyon. Such a lonely sight, and such a shock not to find you there with it. Thank goodness the weather tonight is especially calm. Vivian, Gilbert, and I set the airship down in the canyon without getting blown away. We collected your luggage from amid a clutter of crates full and empty. I was beside myself with worry, to find your luggage but not you!"

"I wasn't worried," Gooper put in.

Tombstone scowled at him. "You was sleepin' off a poison dart."

"Exactly." Gooper's mustache settled into a rueful upward curve.

Joyce snorted in Gooper's direction. "We didn't linger for fear of being late for our rendezvous. We lifted off and flew a spiral search pattern. It wasn't long before we picked up your personal pulse transmitter, Ace. From there, we homed in on you easily."

The corners of Ace's eyes crinkled. "Just in time for Dr. Fairweather's appendectomy. Good work." Ace next regarded the Prince and the young woman. Haltingly, she spoke in their ancient Kush language. Gradually, their story emerged as Ace translated.

"I am Saret, son of Akhen, who was pharaoh in Meroë-inet for many good and fruitful years. Thubis was a high priest. My father died before I came of age. I was crowned Pharaoh as was proper, but the high priests took care of most of the affairs of government and performed most of the rituals. Then, the Englishmen came, and also I met Khontum. This one, Fairweather, was the leader. We had conversations about the wider world and keeping Meroë-inet secret. Or letting the secret out. To be secret forever cannot be, yet to break the secret suddenly would bring nothing but ruin. We did not solve the problem, but our hearts beat together and our minds were in accord.

"But Thubis and the other two Englishmen conspired against me. The Englishmen wanted gold. Thubis wanted to deny me my throne and sit upon it himself. Upon the day I came into inheritance, they blasphemed against the gods. The one called Darby wore a costume like Horus, and the one called Bertram shone a silent, flameless light upon him. The priests treated the man as if he was a manifestation of Horus, and allowed the false Horus to take my sceptre and give it to Thubis. The guards, my own cousins, threw me in the dungeon. Khontum's tears were not heeded, and she was not allowed to see me."

A male voice with a British accent broke in. "Every word of that is true. Saret is a man of honor. It is a privilege to know him."

Everyone swiveled to look at Miles Fairweather. He lay on his operating table, but he was evidently awake judging by his set jaw and studiously resolute expression.

Ace smiled, then said, "Commodore … I mean, Joyce? He'll be dehydrated. Could you get him some water please?" Khontum assisted Joyce Harcourt with the water, pouring from the amphora that she and Saret had brought.

Vivian said from the window, "I see some pre-dawn light, Commodore."

Joyce answered automatically. "Well, we'd better lift, then!"

Ace held up a finger. "One moment. Let me be sure Saret and Khontum are in full accord."

There was a conversation in the ancient tongue. It went on for a minute, then two. Ace's face pinched as if she were biting lemons. Khontum added words. Eventually, Ace's shoulders slumped a little and she nodded, saying, "Ce!"

Immediately, Saret and Khontum flashed grins.

Ace glumly said, "They need back into Khontum's house to get a few things. They're coming with us though. Liftoff in ten minutes."

"Wot was all that, Ace?" Gooper wondered, eyeing her suspiciously.

Ace shook her head in the negative. "Nothing, hopefully. Go with them, Gooper. And Tombstone. I can't shake the feeling we're being watched."

"Yes'm."

Ace swiveled and stepped to the cockpit, really just the front portion of the lounge. It was elevated by one step and bristled with switches, dials, and levers. She made a paradoxical sight. Ace still wore her servant's kalasiri and sandals yet she assumed confident control of the ultramodern dirigible.

Miles Fairweather studied Joyce Harcourt from his reclining position. He cleared his throat. "Might I ask who you are, madam? I must say, this whole affair has been miraculous. Dungeon to deathbed to you. Such a lovely woman. Did they call you 'Commodore?'"

"Oh!" Joyce Harcourt straightened up and smoothed out her flight suit. "Well, I'm not an Air Commodore any more. I'm just Joyce Harcourt. A pleasure to make your acquaintance, sir. Erm, Doctor Fairweather."

"Please, call me Miles."

Ace addressed Vivian and Gilbert. "Exterior inspection, then lift. Ten minutes."

"Yes, Captain."

As Ace headed back to the exit ladder, Saret and Khontum came in bearing hastily assembled bundles. Clothing, it looked like, and plenty of accessories, including several voluminous wigs. Ace shot the bundles an uncomfortable glance as she passed. She quit the gondola in haste, as if escaping from some hidden menace.

Ace paused at the bottom of the ladder to breathe in a few lungfuls of cool desert air. The nearby villa cast an elegant silhouette against the gray dawn. Cornices shaped like the twin plumes of Amun's helm speared into the sky. Quiet lay on the landscape like a blanket of peace. Not even a scarab beetle could walk undetected.

She scanned the landscape for shapes out of place, but saw nothing human. "I guess it was my imagination," she muttered. "We're alone after all. Fine. On to the inspection."

Ace sauntered under the whale-like cloud of the airship, peering up. Her knowing gaze raked the motors, the propellers, the skin, and the control surfaces. The dim light revealed no blemish or irregularity. Her light footfalls crunched loudly on the dry soil.

Ace paused to revel in the silence and solitude … and nearly jumped out of her skin when a sharp voice called, almost at her elbow. The male voice demanded in the ancient tongue of Kush, "You, there! What is this thing?"

Ace whirled to face a man in a shendyt, indistinct under the airship's shadow. His movements were silent as a ghost, and Ace's jaw dropped in amazement. Her own footfalls were booms of a kettledrum in comparison.

"Answer me, servant!"

Ace's mind whirled. There was something familiar about the man. She struggled to reply in Kush, "It is … a bird of—"

"Who are you? I have no servant so tall." The man stepped closer, with footfalls more quiet than a beetle. His dancelike grace contrasted sharply with his brash and severe speech.

As he approached, his sour facial features showed better. Ace gasped. "Bareem?"

"Aiee!" he cried. In an instant, his hand darted to his waist, and in the next a golden flash sparked in his hand. Bareem's gold knife threatened Ace once again.

Ace bounced backward, landing in a crouch. "Peace!" she said in English, then repeated it in Kush.

"You." He all but spat the word. "You never obey." He advanced.

Ace retreated. "Seldom," she corrected. "I seldom obey. But are we enemies? Put away that knife."

"No." He kept coming, and he accelerated. Ace backpedaled faster, always facing Bareem. The man's perpetual scowl deepened as they left the airship's shadow. "You were given to the Englishmen. You should not be here."

"I'm not property!" Anger knit Ace's brow.

A cactus speared her in the ankle, and she tumbled backwards with a yelp. Bareem leapt after her, knife raised high.

Chapter 28

Bareem's lightning-fast slash missed by inches. Ace arched her back and vaulted backwards onto her hands, then performed a handspring. Fortunately, no cactus met her palms as she pushed off.

Bareem hissed.

Ace's feet found ground, and she veered sideways.

"I have seen better. You are no *kekewe-saew*!" he said. Then he spat other vehement words, unfamiliar to Ace but scorching.

Ace sprinted. Bareem pursued.

His speed astounded, but Ace's legs were longer and she could see well enough to avoid tripping hazards. She sprinted for the gondola ladder.

The crew and passengers in the airship heard a thump and felt a vibration in the metal floor. A moment later, a golden blur skidded into the lounge. "Help!" Ace gasped. "And be careful. He's got a knife."

A moment later, he stood on the threshold to the lounge, his face scrunched into a grimace of distaste. His gold knife glittered in his left hand. His feet spread wide in a confident fighting stance. Sheer annoyance locked every muscle in his face, leaving no room for fear.

"Hey, lookit who." Tombstone squared his shoulders.

Gooper's fists balled up into gallon-sized lumps.

But of the airship occupants, Khontum reacted

most violently. Her hands flew to her cheeks and she shrieked, "Eiote!"

Bareem's eyes bugged out and his mouth dropped open. The single word slumped his shoulders and his knife hand wavered. His jaw worked until he managed his own breathy word. "Khontum."

Ace slowly straightened from her own fighting crouch. "Khontum said, 'Father.'"

"Bareem's her father?" Tombstone's brow wrinkled.

Bareem's eyes twitched just left of Khontum. His jaw grew slack again, but he choked out a new word. "Saret!"

Khontum marched over to Bareem, and he did not resist as she removed his knife from his grip and waggled it at him. She erupted into a righteous stream of rapid and indignant verbiage.

The words flew by too fast for Ace to get more than a taste of meaning. Saret looked like he might interrupt for a moment, but then he clamped his mouth shut. He stood like a rock at Khontum's shoulder. The rest of the occupants of the airship exchanged puzzled glances.

Bareem had little to say, and after a half minute raised his hand in a gesture of peace. Khontum stopped talking, touched her opposite shoulder with a hand, and dropped her head in a small bow. For the first time, Bareem's face relaxed into something that might be considered pleasant.

Saret glanced back at the ring of google-eyed foreigners. "All is well," he said.

Bareem stayed behind, saying, "I do not wish to float on the air."

The instant the door closed behind him, Ace all but ran to the front of the gondola. "Lift!" she cried. "The last thing we want is to become a tourist attraction."

"Yes, ma'am," Gilbert replied.

"They're impressively efficient," Joyce Harcourt said, gesturing to encompass the brother and sister team. "And so young."

"Sixteen isn't so young," Ace replied vaguely, drifting to a window and gluing herself there as the airship fell away from the ground.

"Ha!" Harcourt's eyes twinkled. "But you, my dear, were rather exceptional."

A retort died on Ace's lips. She stabbed a finger at the window, angled downward. "I'm not crazy! There's a figure … no, there are two of them. See?"

Mystified, Harcourt peered out the window and down into the gray and shadowy farmland. She squinted. "Yes, I see them. Odd. Decidedly odd. Oh, are those masks? A hawk and a jackal, I suppose they are."

"*Kekewe-saew*," said Saret from the next window down.

At his side, Khontum gave an enraptured coo as the airship lifted. Her eyes roamed the landscape avidly and had little time for mere shadow-dancers.

Ace tore her eyes from the *kekewe-saew* and rested them on Saret. "They followed us."

"Yes," he spoke to the window.

"They did not stop us."

Saret glanced over at Ace. "They did not kill us. It means that the command to kill us was omitted."

"That makes me feel better."

"Omitted *this* night."

"That makes me feel worse."

Saret gazed out the window.

Ace's eyes stayed on Saret. While Ace had been outside tripping over cacti, Khontum had wiped the worst of Saret's grime away and dressed him in a shendyt kilt. His ribs showed, but his bearing was un-bowed.

Ace tapped her chin. "Saret, will Bareem tell the pharaoh about us?"

The prince answered with an air of surety. "Not unless commanded. He was of the *kekewe-saew* that served my father. He is duty-bound to serve the pharaoh, but he has no love for Thubis."

"Oh! Former *kekewe-saew*. That explains a lot," Ace said. She steepled her fingers. "I wonder if he would consider giving me walking lessons."

Saret's brow wrinkled. "You know how to walk."

"Not like he does."

They nestled the airship in a small side-canyon miles away from Meroë-inet. Everyone caught up on news and napped. They waited for the revealing day-light to pass, so that they could return to Meroë-inet under cover of darkness.

Toward evening, Saret and Khontum captured Ace.

They dragged her into the largest cabin and closed the door. A few groans from Ace and many happy coos and giggles from Khontum leaked from behind the door.

Meanwhile, Miles Fairweather begged to shave off over a month's worth of beard. An amused Joyce Harcourt found a basin and a razor and lathered his face with soap. She set to work.

Half a beard later, Ace emerged from the cabin, pushed from behind by the prince and his bride.

There was a chorus of "Ohhhhh!!!" from the small crowd in the lounge.

"Isis!" Miles Fairweather breathed.

"Resplendent!" Gooper gasped.

Ace's chagrined facial expression notwithstanding, the rest of her was gloriously bedecked in gold and white. Across her shoulders lay a sparkling mantle. Atop her head was a spectacular headdress often seen in statuary depicting Isis. The sun-and-horns icon symbolic of abundant life shone in gold leaf on top. Underneath the helm lay an abundance of black wig arranged in helical curls. Iridescent makeup accentuated her eyes, brows, and lips.

Ace whined, "They want me to play the part of Isis and take the Helm of Amun from Thubis and crown Saret with it!"

Glances were exchanged.

Tombstone said, "Not a bad idea!"

"Bloody brilliant, really," Gooper put in.

Ace spluttered, "It's … it's … well, it's not honest!"

Joyce Harcourt glanced penetratingly at Ace, then gestured with her razor. "That the very thought of being honest occurred to you does you great credit, Ace.

But do look at it pragmatically. Can you think of an easier way to do justice? The alternative, well the only alternative I can think of, is if Saret attempts a coup. That sounds grim. People will die. It might even lead to civil war."

Tombstone waggled a thumb at Ace. "Miz Harcourt, ma'am? She jes' thinks dresses are sissy."

"Well, I'm certainly outvoted." The unhappy frown lingered on Ace's face.

"Seein' as 'ow you're a Yank, you've got ter submit tew th' will of th' majority." Gooper grinned.

Saret spoke. Ace interpreted in resigned tones. "He says he knows of a secret passage to and from an alcove just behind the pharaoh's throne."

"Well, that's perfect!" Joyce said, laughing.

"All right. I'm not enthusiastic, but I'll do it," Ace said.

There was a round of applause.

Tombstone did not participate. His long face grew faraway. He rubbed at his stubbly chin with finger and thumb. As the others threw him quizzical glances, he drawled, "Gooper? Ace? I've got one more ten-dollar word for ya."

"What word, guv?" Gooper asked.

"Bioluminescence."

The problem of method was perhaps solved, but the matter of timing was a complete unknown. Thubis, the high priests, and as many witnesses as possible needed to be in one place at one time. That implied some sort of ritual gathering. Perhaps Sam could tell them when such a thing might happen. In any case, Sam needed rescuing from the Entwhistle brothers' villa. The villa that had belonged to High Priest Hut-Met only yesterday.

The party set out before sunset, leaving the airship manned by Fairweather, Harcourt, Vivian, and Gilbert. Gooper carried the suitcase-radio in case they needed to call the airship. Tombstone carried another bag with the Isis costume in it, including also a pair of test tubes from Gooper's collection. The tubes contained chemicals that, when mixed, would glow in gentle amber.

Ace, back in her servant's kalsiri, carried a coil of rope over her shoulder.

Gooper and Tombstone wore hastily-butchered sheets and safety pins. In dim light, the improvised shendyts might roughly conform to local dress code. In bright light, they were doomed anyway, being light of skin and also far too large (Gooper horizontally and Tombstone vertically). Gooper was so pale that they dusted him with dirt to try to decrease his reflectivity. Judging by his drooping mustache, he felt rather melancholy about the whole thing. Tombstone's laughter did nothing to lighten his mood.

Saret and Khontum were both dressed in their own noble clothes. Khontum rolled the hem of her kalasiri higher so she could swing her legs more athletically.

They hiked up and over a ridge that separated them from the main valley of Meroë-inet. Long grasses, sparse and browned, softened the arid outlines of the stark canyonscape. They twice disturbed small herds of dik-diks. The knee-high antelope bounced away, sometimes leaping head-high as they fled the walkers. Gooper pointed out a cheetah atop a distant rock. It lazily and regally tracked the slow procession of humans.

As the last rays of sunlight slanted across the savannah, Gooper emitted a breathy gasp of astonishment. He crouched and pointed. There was a pair of large antelope trotting toward them. High, muscular front shoulders sloped down to rear hips. Their horns were shaped almost identically to the sun-and-horns emblem of Isis. Gooper said in hushed tones, "There they are! Look at 'em! Tora hartebeests, they're called. Rarest of the rare! I thought I'd live an' die and never see one! Cor! Lookit! Pinch me! Am I dreaming?"

Tombstone forgot entirely to insult Gooper. He said, softly, "Beautiful!"

Saret and Khontum seized this moment to squeeze each other while gazing at the antelope.

"Wonderful," Ace agreed softly.

The sun set.

They continued on, crossing the ridge and descending into the hidden valley.

CHAPTER 29

The walled villa loomed, dark and quiet. Ace tossed a loop of rope over a stone plume where two walls met. She whisked up with such ease it seemed as if gravity switched directions for her. Silhouetted for a moment on top of the wall, she flipped the rope to the inside and disappeared into the courtyard.

The rest of the nervous party twitched in a huddle outside.

Ten minutes later, a soft plop startled them. But it was Ace. She landed crouched, then rose and coiled her rope. "I see only strangers dressed like servants." She pointed to the front door. "Let's have Saret try the front door."

"Eh? Wot if those Entwhistle brothers are hiding, waiting to pounce?" Gooper whispered.

Ace shrugged the coiled rope back over her shoulder. "I doubt I'm expected, but there might be some kind of trap, yes. We must be cautious."

Saret and Khontum hailed at the front door. Ace and her associates lurked out of sight, flanking the front door, rigid with the tension of what might happen next.

But when the door opened, only ordinary conversation ensued back and forth. Ace puzzled out a translation.

"Hello?"

"Good evening. May Nut Skymother protect you this night."

"May you walk in the shadow of the Hidden God."

"Are the Englishmen at home?"

"No, friend. They have gone to the execution."

"And which execution is that?"

"You don't know? Everyone knows. It is their slave, Sam. He who aided the escape of the prisoners." The servant gasped and spoke over himself. "Wait! Are you——?"

Saret chuckled. "Yes, I am Saret! And what say you to that, my friend?"

The servant's voice muffled, as if suddenly speaking through a pillow. Ace snuck a peek. She blinked. The fellow had prostrated himself at the feet of Saret and Khontum. "Prince Saret! O glory! You have returned!"

"Let us say, I shall return shortly if Isis grants me her blessing. For now, I would ask you please to keep this meeting quiet for a little while. I am sure there are some that hunt me."

"Prince Saret, I will be silent! May Isis grant you her wings!"

"I hope she does, my friend. I shall need speed. Farewell."

"Farewell! Hurry, if you wish to see the execution. It is at moonset."

Saret and Khontum strode away hand in hand. The front door closed. Ace, Gooper, and Tombstone followed the couple. As they entered the main road, they accelerated until they were loping along at a run. It was only then that Gooper and Tombstone learned that Sam was to be executed.

"Moonset?" Gooper said. "But there's the crescent

moon, right there! It's halfway down the sky already!"

Tombstone said, "Gooper. That's why we're *running* right now! I wish I had my horse."

"Oh, ha, ha. D'you still 'ave the Isis costume?"

"Yep. You still got the radio?"

"Aye."

"We must go to the royal apartments," said Saret, whose words Ace relayed to Gooper and Tombstone. "That is walled, too, with walls higher than a house. There might be guards. Traditionally, the guards are the *kekewe-saew*, the shadow assassins, the guardians of darkness. They have a strict code of honor. They love me, but they may not be able to obey me. I do not know what Thubis may have ordered."

"Shadow assassins?" Tombstone huffed as he ran.

Saret explained a bit more, "The *kekewe-saew* have the blessing of Nephthys. As her agents, they have authority to send undeserving souls to the underworld. They are also dancers and entertainers for the pharaoh. If one sees the shadow dancers, despite the beauty of their motions, one knows that death, the kiss of Nephthys, will follow shortly. One can only hope death comes for some other and not him!"

"The secret way goes from the apartments to the temple?" Ace asked.

"Yes," huffed Saret, who now needed all his breath for running.

But the temple was close already. Drum beats and bell clangs wafted on the evening air. The streets and staircases were empty. Saret steered them to one side, to a walled enclosure. Ace did not ask or wait. She lassoed the right-hand pillar of the tall, decorated gate and swarmed over the top.

Moments later, a heavy scrape sound signaled the unbarring of the gate. It smoothly opened on big brass hinges. Ace shrugged and displayed empty hands. She had seen no one.

Saret and Khontum led the way into the royal apartments with sure feet. They banged open an interior door and ran in. It was lit on the inside by oil lamps. There was a feminine shriek. Saret and Khontum ran back out again, pursued by two men carrying spears with leaf-shaped bronze heads.

"Oh, yeah!" Gooper said gleefully, stepping in to lay hands on the spear from one guard.

"I hear you, Gooper," Tombstone drawled, doing likewise to the other.

They tussled, growling and shuffling for footing. Ace circled the fight, face scrunched in worry. Unpredictable slashes of the razor-sharp spear blades kept her from leaping in to assist. Gooper and Tombstone fought for position. Grunts of strength pitted against strength echoed in the stony room.

Gooper and Tombstone gained the outside, and by degrees pushed the guards back to back. "One. Two," wheezed Gooper. "Three," added Tombstone. On cue, the associates pushed with the shafts of the spears. The guards' heads met with loud wooden reports. The guards relaxed instantly, slithering to the floor in boneless piles. Gooper and Tombstone examined their new weapons, and Ace darted in to assess the condition of the unconscious guards.

All five of them then crept into the lamplit apartment.

There was a woman standing, fearful but erect, by a thick, dangling rope. The colorful rope ascended through a hole in the ceiling. It looked like a bell-pull.

She said something in the ancient tongue.

Ace blew air out of puffed cheeks. Her shoulders slumped. "She said it is too late. She already called the *kekewe-saew*."

Saret said a few words, and the woman's fear-filled eyes relaxed a trifle.

In utter silence, they came in from the far door, running on bare feet. There were no god-masks, but their faces were painted an eerie jet black. They each carried a knife, slender and deadly. There were eight of them. In a few seconds, they spread out, surrounding the party. Gooper and Tombstone froze, keeping a hold on their new spears. Ace stared at Saret.

Saret remained outwardly calm, holding hands with Khontum. He spoke several sentences.

There was a tableau in which no one moved a muscle. Hammer-pulses of blood rushed in their eardrums.

Then, all eight *kekewe-saew* reversed their knives and knelt, offering the hilts to Saret. The eyes of the woman who had summoned them widened, and one of her hands flew to her mouth in shocked surprise.

Saret pivoted, touching each hilt. He spoke a few more words to the *kekewe-saew*, and they melted into a semicircle behind him. He glanced at Ace and spoke a single word.

Ace groaned. "Nuts. It's Isis time."

Chapter 30

Banners depicting the siblings Nephthys, Osiris, Isis, and Seth decorated the temple courtyard. A cluster of musicians beat drums, tapped tambourines, plucked harps, and blew double-oboes.

Despite the musicians and banners, the people of Meroë-inet were subdued. The criminal, Sam, was a stranger to them. His punishment, death, seemed out of proportion to his crime: letting another stranger walk free. Furthermore, the swift whispered rumors were that Prince Saret had escaped along with the other prisoners who broke out of the royal dungeon. This, more than anything, was the topic of conversation. They called him "the crocodile-kissed prince" and spoke of him yearningly.

Sam heard much of it. He was chained to a pole in the courtyard, raised on a small stage. Traditionally, he should be taunted and jeered at during this phase of the ritual, but he was largely left alone. Indeed, Sam felt that he was in an invisible bubble, inside of which no one came, or spoke.

The pole at Sam's back fit in the center hole of a stone disk. At his feet, twenty-four carved rays formed a starburst among a jumble of hieroglyphs. Half the disk represented the realm of Geb and the other half Nut. Day and night. Life and death. The endless cycle of time.

Sam's eyes flicked right to his sarcophagus. The

roughly-made box barely resembled the gold-inlaid masterpieces crafted for dead nobility. A heavy lid swung on crude bronze hinges. Both lid and back bristled with inward-pointing brass spikes.

When ritual permitted, the lid would close on him. Pierced by many nails, he would die over the course of hours in horrible agony in the claustrophobic darkness. More importantly in the minds of the citizens of Meroë-inet, Sam's soul could never make the journey to the underworld while the spikes nailed it in place. This fact held more horror than the brutal nature of the killing because it was a true ending. Even the hand of Nephthys could not bring Sam's soul away.

From minute to minute Sam careened between heart-hammering panic and exhausted resignation.

The thought of his friends rescuing him had occurred to him, but the steady, inexorable ritual had worn hope to almost nothing. Hour after hour dragged by. Tied to a great wheel of fate, unwilling Sam churned to his untimely end with agonizing slowness.

Shouting defiance did not appeal to him. Nor did weeping. Instead, he numbly listened to nearby conversation and the heavy throbbing of the ritual drums. Details in the banners and wall carvings sifted through his Egyptologist's mind.

The broad temple courtyard was arranged so that all eyes would gravitate forward. From Sam's courtyard location, six broad steps led to a higher plane, flanked by statues of Isis, goddess of birth, and Nephthys, goddess of death. On that higher level were the pharaoh's dais and throne, set before a massive archway. Past the arch stood a wall covered in historical hieroglyphs and images.

Pharaoh Thubis left his throne and waddled forward. His retinue came with him: scribes and servants and high priests, four to the left and four to the right. The Entwhistle brothers straggled along in the right-hand group, dressed as if going on safari. Darby seemed sunk in misery and Bertram looked gloomy as well. Perhaps they were realizing for the first time that being high priests had certain drawbacks. Attending lengthy rituals such as this one, for example. Constant obedience to the pharaoh differed vastly from freedom.

Sam sneered at the Englishmen. His tiny gesture of defiance may have been invisible in the dim light of the flaming braziers, but it made Sam feel slightly more himself.

The pharaoh seemed nervous and impatient though he had not been there long. He wore the Helm of Amun and carried the crook scepter of the pharaoh. He glanced at Sam, and Sam drew himself as tall as possible. Sam saw shadowy movement behind the dais and throne by the huge arch.

The pharaoh pointed at the drummers and chopped with his hand in the air. The music cut off. The murmurs of the crowd tapered to a whisper. The committee of executioners closed in on Sam. Callused hands encircled his upper arms as others worked to remove his bronze chains.

The time had come for Sam to enter his coffin of torture.

Tombstone raced down the secret stairs three at a time, all elbows and knees. His dour face grimaced in alarm. He landed at the bottom, almost plowing into a *kekewe-saew*. "They're puttin' Sam in a box full o' nails! They're gonna skewer him to death! I think mebbe they already did it. I din't watch, I came down here, instead."

Khontum and Saret lifted a gracefully-horned tiara in the air, affixing it to a cascade of black hair. From under the wig Ace spluttered, "What? But it's not moonset yet!"

Gooper paled under his dirt. "Blimey! Say it isn't so."

Ace spoke in Kush, urging Saret and Khontum to hurry.

Tombstone reversed directions, climbing the steps one by one, each footfall heavy with dread. "Poor Sam. Poor ol' Sam."

Murmurs raced through the crowd as the anticipation of spilt blood sharpened. A disapproving voice cut through. "The moon has not yet set!"

Bareem stood in front of the spiked coffin. His arms folded across his chest and his signature scowl framed glaring eyes fixed on Thubis.

A ripple swept the crowd. Thubis's froglike eyes roved until they found Bareem. "What? It is close enough."

Bareem stood as if carved of grumpy granite. "Death comes in the darkness. It seems that *some* high priests have forgotten the symbols. Or perhaps never learned them." Bareem's glare swiveled to the Englishmen.

Neither Englishman spoke the language. They could only stand silently as a hundred eyes turned toward them. Firelight reflected from their pale foreheads as nervous sweat sprang from their skin.

Pharaoh Thubis watched the Englishmen, too, an unpleasant smile curling his lips. But a moment later, he waved his hand dismissively in the air. "Bareem, you speak correctly, but we must forgive small errors. It is close enough. So say I, Thubis, Pharaoh of Meroë-inet."

Bareem remained a statue for a moment. Nearby guards eyed him speculatively. Would the veteran official dare to defy a direct dismissal? Perhaps more blood than that of the stranger would be spilled this night.

But Bareem bent at the waist and spread his arms in a graceful bow of acceptance. Bareem stepped away from the sarcophagus, and the guards flanking Sam pushed and pulled him toward the spiky box. Dull nails clawed at Sam's shoulder blade as he stumbled. A whimper escaped his lips.

"Isis preserve me," he whispered. Thubis stared avidly at him, as if Sam were a lobster about to be cooked for dinner.

"Finish it," Thubis commanded.

Thubis's hungry expression fascinated Sam, but more movement by the throne caught Sam's attention. Saret and Khontum marched in from behind the throne into the firelight. They also came chained. *Kekewe-saew* in god-masks held the free ends of the chains and crept forward in sinuous silence. The crowd behind him erupted in a buzz of excited whispers.

The executioners flanking Sam loosened their grip in order to grasp and slam closed the spiky coffin lid. But they, too, turned to stare at Saret, Khontum, and the *kekewe-saew*.

The last to see was Thubis. He narrowed bulging eyes at the crowd, then heaved around to behold the sight. He inhaled sharply and splayed his fingers out in a warding gesture. Sam could only imagine his dumbfounded facial expression.

Despite having chains around his wrists, Saret was dressed richly. Bangles and rings sparkled aplenty but no headdress graced his curls. Displaying none of the dejection of a prisoner in chains, he stood on solid legs. He raised his young voice to carry through the crowd.

"Saret, son of Akhen, Pharaoh of Meroë-inet, is returned. The great Isis walks with me. Yes, Isis herself came to bring me out of my stony cell to the free air. But now, I am captured once again. What will you do, Thubis?"

The crowd shivered and thrilled at the sacrilege of omitting Thubis's title of pharaoh. There was a collective low, yearning, breathy sound from those gathered. Sam was all but forgotten, though his arms were still gripped by his motionless executioners.

Keenly aware of the insult, Thubis spluttered something. To Sam, it sounded like, "I am Pharaoh! My word is law!" Thubis happened to be wearing a small dagger, a ceremonial dagger shaped like a wavy snake. He drew it and stepped toward Saret and Khontum.

Darby Entwhistle said distinctly in English, "Wait. They're not actually shackled! They're not tied up!" But few hearing his words understood the alien language.

Saret shouted, "O Isis! Save me!"

At that moment, bronze lids clapped down on the two braziers that flanked the throne itself. Showers of sparks erupted as the flames extinguished. The throne area dimmed into a deeper gloom. Sam blinked his eyes and furrowed his brow. The two that did the fire-snuffing, though indistinct, had looked like Gooper and Tombstone.

Suddenly, a sunburst of joy flamed through Sam's veins. His fingers slowly curled to form fists.

But the crowd let out a louder moan of, "Ohhhhhh!" They had seen something new.

The luminous figure strolled from behind the throne. In a few steps, she stood just behind Thubis, towering over him. Her rich raiment glistened with gold and sparkling bangles, and the sun-and-horns on her headdress gleamed. Even her skin glowed radiantly, stretched over flowing muscles.

"Isis!" a few voices called from the crowd.

"Isis!" cried Sam. Tears sprang to his eyes. His heart leapt at the sight of goddess and he half-sobbed again, "Isis! O Isis!"

Isis's stern face glowed, her attention fixed upon cosmic infinity. One arm raised, its finger extended. The glowing arm swiveled to Saret and Khontum. Immediately, their chains fell from them to clatter metallically on the ground.

Over the excited burbling of the crowd Sam's sharp ears heard Darby exclaim, "Bloody hell! That's *my* trick!"

Bertram yammered, "What do we do? What do we do?"

The *kekewe-saew* assumed dancelike poses. The crowd of citizens began to slowly move toward the throne area as if ensorcelled.

"No! No!" shouted Thubis. His eyes stared on the brink of madness. He pointed his ornamental dagger at Saret and frantically commanded, "*Kekewe-saew!* Kill!"

But Isis had other ideas. She strode one long step and swept her hand forward to grip Thubis by the throat. With the other hand, she encircled Thubis's dagger hand and gave it a seemingly-gentle shake. The ornamental knife clattered to the floor.

Saret and Khontum moved toward the crowd, ignoring Thubis's struggles.

Sam's eye was caught by a metallic glint off to the right side. He squinted to focus. It was Darby, raising a pistol and aiming at Isis. Sam shouted, "Look out!"

But Isis was busy. One luminous hand pressed into Thubis's neck and the other lifted the Helm of Amun from his head. The goddess's eyes glanced at Darby as the gun zeroed in on her. There was no time to do anything else.

But the priest next to Darby moved. He, too, had a ceremonial dagger. He arced it downwards across Darby's gun arm. His arm deflected down and to the side. The gun popped and puffed smoke.

Darby cried out in pain and anger and turned on the priest next to him. It was Hut-Met whose house had been taken over by Darby and Bertram. Darby raised his gun and aimed it between Hut-Met's eyes. But the *kekewe-saew* danced near. Tiny flickers of movement danced in the mouths of the jesters' masks. Darby seemed to forget his murderous intent. His stance wobbled. His gun-wielding arm dropped. A few seconds later, Darby and Bertram toppled to the ground.

The crowd twitched when the gun went off, but Saret raised his arms, one of which was holding Khontum's. "My friends! My people! I am delivered by Isis who has come again to give aid!"

Isis let Thubis drop insensate to the stones and held the Helm of Amun high in the air.

The crowd began to chant, "Saret! Saret! Saret!"

Saret and Khontum held their pose for long moments. Then, they dropped their hands. Saret turned and knelt with due ceremony before Isis.

As he was crowned, the crowd cheered.

Chapter 31

Saret and Khontum posed once again after the crowning, arms raised in victory. Sam shrugged out of the grip of his executioners, and they did not resist. Sam and Bareem exchanged glances. Sam bowed to him, and he harrumphed, but warmth softened his otherwise black scowl.

Isis turned her back on the affair and disappeared into the arch behind the throne. Hidden doors to the left and to the right connected to stairs, and the royal apartments. Gooper and Tombstone slunk down the steps after her. They paused at the first lit lamp to breathe.

"All my nerves are wracked!" Tombstone said, shaking his head.

"I find it hard to believe actors somehow *like* this sort of thing," Ace grumbled.

Gooper gestured in agitation. "At least yew look good. That chemical glow is amazing! To the contrary, I'm covered in grit wearing a skirt."

Ace said, with a pang of concern, "I hope someone notices the blood. Darby shot Thubis. He was aiming for me, but Hut-Met deflected his gun."

"We were in time to save Sam. I can't scrape up any sympathy fer Darby or Thubis or Bertram. They dug their latrine. Now they're buried in—"

"Tombstone, be nice!" Ace shushed him.

Two days later, the airship docked at the Egyptian stylized Stonehenge by the lake. It was the hour of departure. Quite a few things had been settled. The stolen necklaces, bracelets, and rings were aboard the *Sky Arrow One*. They had been stolen, not only from Devonshire, but also from Monte Carlo by Bertram Entwhistle. Hut-Met found the jewels in a small chest in his villa when he returned to inhabit it along with his household.

Darby and Bertram would not be travelling to face justice in Monte Carlo or Devonshire any time soon. First, they were to serve their sentences for their local crimes as laborers of the lowest caste. Since Pharaoh Saret did not mention any time limit, the brothers might be calling Meroë-inet home for a long, long time.

Thubis lay convalescent. His thigh bullet wound was serious, but Ace thought it likely he would recover. His judgment would come "later" according to Saret.

Another casualty appeared to be Tombstone's hat and boots. Those items never surfaced.

Ace kept out of sight for the most part, but she wasn't idle. With help from Khontum, she persuaded a reluctant Bareem to give her a lesson in walking silently.

Polite gawkers loitered near the *Sky Arrow One*, including a small group of apprentice scribes. They sketched it from their various vantage points, recording their impressions on clay tablets. Vivian and Gilbert stayed near the airship. They, in turn, gawked at the scribes and sightseers. Wonder-filled smiles seldom left their faces.

Sam and Ace stood in the stone circle, Ace in her customary flight suit and Sam in a neat shendyt that was a gift from Khontum.

"I think the Egyptians have behaved most nobly regarding the jewels," Sam remarked. "I can see how the sight of the gems ignites flames of desire in their eyes, yet they gave them up to us. It is their world. There would be no repercussions if they were to forget their honor."

"I agree, Sam. On the subject of honor, however, do you think that 'Isis' really fooled anybody? Or do you think that the people wanted Saret to be pharaoh and went along with the charade?"

Sam considered the question, glancing at the lake, and the hillside palace, and the airship, and finally Ace. He smoothed his curled mustache. "It does not matter. Personally speaking, Ace, even my heart was overwhelmed at the sight of Isis appearing from thin air. Consider any person with some romance in their hearts. Surely they, like me, would yearn for Isis to be real, even if a corner of their logical heart advised otherwise. And if their hearts are entirely cold and dispassionate, then, as you say, they would prefer the consensus of the many. They would crave the comfort of tradition. In all ways, Saret is preferred over Thubis."

"Sam." Ace's voice dropped so low she almost whispered. "This is strange, but in that moment when Darby was aiming his gun at me, I felt like a goddess. I felt at peace. I felt invulnerable. It was all distinctly …

irrational."

Sam smoothed his mustache curl. "Pay it no mind, memsahib. It was the stress."

"Indeed. Good point." Ace unnecessarily smoothed out the fabric on her flight suit sleeves. "Look. The farewell party is coming."

The royal procession approached from the palace. The resplendent company came more slowly than they otherwise would have, perhaps. Miles Fairweather set the pace, and he followed doctor's orders to move with care for his recovery. His arm linked with Joyce Harcourt's. Both were impeccably attired in local dress. The pair led the procession with great dignity.

Tombstone in his western shirt and (spare) cowboy boots and Gooper in his suit and cap ambled over from the airship.

Everyone bowed for Saret and Khontum.

After a round of sunny greetings, Ace narrowed her eyes at the pair of older English folk. "Dr. Fairweather. Commodore Harcourt. You are coming with us?"

The pair grinned widely as they shook their heads no. Joyce answered, "Maybe later. We have been invited to be ambassadors to Meroë-inet. We have decided to accept that solemn responsibility."

Miles said, "It'll be tricky business, opening up the valley. It must be done by those who love it and care for it. People who understand both its grandeur and its fragility."

Joyce added, "And there's no particular rush. I need to learn the language."

Ace said, "Well, I think that's very noble of you. Congratulations!"

Miles and Joyce smiled at Ace, then at each other.

Their hands met and clasped.

191

192

CHAPTER 32

"Lovey dovey Brits!" drawled Tombstone in the lounge of *Sky Arrow One*. They rose effortlessly above Meroë-inet. From the air, the lake and valley transformed into a blue-green gem set in a crown of ivory and gold.

"Yew 'ave no idea, stick-man!" Gooper grinned.

"Hush, you walrus. I've seen you dressed in sheets. A description could be leaked to the papers any time I choose."

"I will nobly ignore that, my ignorant companion from backward Texas, for I 'ave seen the tora hartebeest. No mere empty threat can subtract from that singular scintillating truth! I'm glad we took this trip!" Gooper glanced over at Sam. "An' glad to find Sam, too."

"Truly, I am humbled and grateful that you have traveled so many thousands of miles to come find me," Sam said.

"Aw, shucks. It's what friends are for," Tombstone drawled.

Gooper called up to the flight cabin. "Ace! Where are we going?"

Ace's voice drifted back. "Who cares? We're flying!"

194

Herald

LONDON, TUESDAY, JULY 11, 1922   TWOPENCE

SUZANNE v. PATTERSON

Why Should They Not Play a Match?

A BRAIN WAVE

Mlle. Lenglen, by her decisive victory over Mrs. Mallory, the American, on Saturday, at Wimbledon, retained the proud title of woman tennis champion of the world.

Late yesterday afternoon Gerald Patterson, the Australian, beating Randolph Lycett, England's last White Hope, again became the champion of the world of men.

Now (writes a tennis correspondent to the DAILY HERALD) how about a match between Mlle. Lenglen and Mr. Patterson for the REAL world's championship?

THE IDEA!

That seems to me to be the natural sequence to the battles which have placed these two players on their separate pedestals, and should provide the battle supreme.

We have seen how much superior they have both been to all the opponents pitted against them in singles.

And Mlle. Lenglen is just as much in a class by herself among the women as Mr. Patterson is among the men.

But there is a difference in the play of both when they are figuring in mixed doubles which is hard to define—a something temperamental, perhaps, which makes such a match as I suggest here all the more intriguing.

A POPULAR EVENT

I discussed such a match yesterday with several ardent tennis "fans," and the divergency of the views expressed convinces me that, in a purely sporting sense, such a match would prove a huge draw, and would furnish connoisseurs in styles with something to exercise their minds.

In any case, your readers' views on the suggested match would, I think, be interesting.

RESCUES FROM A PRECIPICE

STOLEN JEWELRY RETURNED

DELIVERED BY AIRSHIP

MISSING ARCHAEOLOGIST FOUND

Echoing her exploit in the Great War, American flying ace Cecilia Carroway landed an airship in London, this time in the courtyard of the British Museum. The lighter-than-air dirigible stayed only long enough to disgorge missing archaeologist Dr. Sam Biming of the British Museum and a small chest. The latter contained jewelry stolen three weeks ago from Fitzhugh Manor near Salisbury.

In contrast to the Ottoman X-8 she landed in 1918, the airship that landed yesterday presumably was not stolen. It bore the letters CARROWAY AERONAUTICS on its tail. Sam Biming was also on the X-8. He had been a code breaker during the war.

The jewel heist set Devon and Somerset counties abuzz. Evidence at the time indicated that a team of children scaled the wall without a ladder, and entered through a window. They stole only a sample of the whole collection, and left a gold ankh of ancient Egyptian styling in its place. A gold ankh of similar style was left in the British Museum when an Egyptian helmet was stolen. A third ankh was recovered in London by Cleopatra's needle.

TWO TWO'S 10 TIMES

Recorder's Remarkable Dates

HIS LUCKY NUMBER

From Our Own Correspondent

BANBURY, Monday — Mr. H. S. Staveley, at Banbury Quarter Sessions to-day, bade farewell to the borough, having resigned the Recordership on being appointed County Court judge for Northamptonshire.

He remarked that people said there was nothing in numbers, but he had a curious history connected with number 22.

He was born on the 22nd day of the month, christened on the 22nd, married on the 22nd, his two children were born on the 22nd, he was called to the Bar on the 22nd, appointed Recorder of Banbury on the 22nd, his appointment as County Court judge was dated the 22nd, and his wife had reminded him that this year was 1922.

This is not all, for 22 still pursues the ex-Recorder. He made his statement at Banbury Quarter Sessions—count the letters in these three words, and—22 again!

"WHY I FLED"—BEVAN

Wife Implored Him to Spare Her Disgrace

VIENNA, Monday.—In response to a request for a statement of his case, Mr. Gerard Lee Bevan has said: "I left England on February 8 solely at the request of my wife, who had information to the effect that a warrant would be issued for my arrest on the following day, and begged and implored me to spare her the disgrace. In her interests, therefore, and those of my family, I consented to go away, though very much against my own will and judgment."—Reuter.

DEATH OF BOW-ST. MAGISTRATE

NOTES

As of the date of this writing, the tora hartebeest remains a real denizen of Eritrea and Ethiopia. If there ever was a time when the tora hartebeest was not elusive and rarely seen, that time is not remembered. Now the rarest of the rare, this large antelope is critically endangered. It has become locally extinct in Sudan, the region of fictional Meroë-Inet. None exist in captivity, either. With only two hundred of the animals left, the magnificent species hangs by a thread, to be cut at the whim of poachers or stretched into nothingness by habitat loss.

I shudder to think of writing a fictional end to a species. Alas, the real world is harder and darker than the bottom limits of my scruples.

As regards the transatlantic voyage of *Sky Arrow One*, it comes late compared to reality. Airships beat heavier-than-air craft for distance and altitude in the early decades of the 20th century, and the first (and second) transatlantic flights took place in 1919.

Imagine if you will the British airship R34: two football fields long, a crew of 26, five engines, and a lot of hydrogen. Mustered for an east-to-west transatlantic journey, it departed Britain on 2 July 1919 and arrived at Long Island on 6 July after a flight of 108 hours. Two stowaways had snuck on board. Crew member William Ballantyne had been ordered to stay home to save weight, but he did not obey. He brought the ship's mascot with him, a tabby kitten named Wopsie. To smooth the process of mooring with a ground crew of inexperienced Americans, one Major Pritchard donned a parachute and jumped from the airship. Undamaged after the drop, he organized the American ground crew and the R34 moored safely. After a four-day layover, R34 reversed course and flew back to England. With the wind, it took only 75 hours.

A little historical accounting may be in order as regards

"firsts."

Alcock and Brown made the first west-to-east Atlantic crossing in June 1919, from Newfoundland, Canada, to Galway, Ireland. The South Atlantic was bridged in 1922. Charles Lindberg's famous 1927 flight chased a slightly different goal: the endpoints were specified as New York and continental Europe.

East-to-west, the R34's 1919 flight remained unchallenged by heavier-than-air craft until Beryl Markham flew it in 1936. By that time, a transatlantic airship service was in full operation. The LZ 127 *Graf Zeppelin* entered commercial service in 1928 and operated until 1937 with various side trips such as a round-the-world jaunt in 1929. Its bread-and-butter run was to ferry passengers between Germany and Brazil.

We're early by a few years for the concept of "air traffic control," but Croydon Airport was Britain's foremost and busiest aerodrome. Among the many historic events that happened at Croydon was the invention of the international distress call "Mayday!" in 1923. I am sorely tempted to fictionalize that event and blame it on Gooper.

And what about Ace? Never one to rest long, our dauntless heroine will shrug off her perilous brush with *acting* and return in her next adventure, *Ace Carroway and the Deadly Violin*. Do you not think that violins can be deadly? Wait until you hear the ghostly tale of violinist P. Charles Derkin, if indeed he can speak it through his chattering teeth.

ABOUT THE AUTHOR

Wyoming native, Guy Worthey, traded spurs and lassos for telescopes and computers when he decided on astrophysics for a day job. Whenever he temporarily escapes the gravitational pull of stars and galaxies, he writes fiction. He lives in Washington state with his violinist wife, Diane. He likes cats and dogs and plays keyboards and bass guitar. His favorite food is called creamed eggs on toast, but once in a while he heeds the siren song of chocolate.

ACKNOWLEDGMENTS

Especial thanks to readers extraordinaire Jess, Sonya, and Tory. Love and gratefulness to my family, especially Diane.

Book 1

Ace Carroway and the Great War

Book 2

Ace Carroway Around the World

Book 3

Ace Carroway and the Handsome Devil

Book 4

Ace Carroway and the Growling Death

Book 5

Ace Carroway and the Midnight Scream

Book 6

Ace Carroway and the Deadly Violin

guyworthey.net

www.ingramcontent.com/pod-product-compliance
Lightning Source LLC
Chambersburg PA
CBHW070949190726
48292CB00004B/1396